NO TIME FOR DAYDREAMS

JAYNE KINGSLEY

To my gorgeous and supportive husband, may we always make time for cake.

ABOUT THIS BOOK

Bekka Arden is determined to turn Something Blue Designs into New York's most sought after Bridal boutique. Jilted just three days before her own wedding, she's now more than happy creating other brides dream dresses. Until her ex's best friend arrives back in town for his sister's wedding. A wedding featuring her dress. And for some reason he keeps on trying to lure her to wedding planning events. Especially tempting planning events, like cake tasting.

But temptation is the entire point. Australian boutique hotelier Noah Fox has struggled to forget Bekka. Having lost his chance with her back in college, he's not throwing away this new opportunity to set her straight about the man he really is: her perfect match. After five years of growing the family business, he's now in New York to show Bekka that he's her something old AND new.

His sister's wedding preparation provides the perfect backdrop for romance, but when a family emergency calls Noah home to Sydney, these two are left with the ultimate choice. Can he help Bekka see that in their game of love, you can have your cake and eat it too?

ABOUT THE AUTHOR

Jayne Kingsley writes contemporary romance filled with fashionable and fun heroines and the hunky heroes that capture their hearts. She currently resides on the picturesque south coast of NSW with her two young daughters and her own real-life gorgeous hero.

She loves connecting with her readers. Head to www.jaynekingsley.com to sign up to her newsletter, or join her official facebook page.

CHAPTER 1

Bekka Arden hopped onto the sidewalk, sipping at her caramel mocha latte. It was her Thursday morning treat from the cafe around the corner and today she needed to make the most of the sugar-laced caffeine. Her heels clicked deliciously against the pavement, her stride bringing her closer to her studio and home and another day of living out her dreams.

Two men in suits passed her, completing a double-take. She heard a low-breathed whistle that pulled the corners of her pale pink lips wide and gave her step extra bounce. This part of Manhattan often had its fair share of businessmen and traders, venturing out of their natural Wall Street habitat in search of lighter air and, in her opinion, better coffee options.

Heading around the last corner, she came to a halt outside her little boutique. It's pristine white trim full-length windows showcased her latest bridal collection. The sun glinted off the pearls on the neckline of her Lisa dress, its tulle skirts sprouting out from the waist and cascading in waves. She cocked her head. Perhaps it was time to jazz up the window a little. Maybe some watercolor floral decals as window borders, or some props? Simplicity and elegance were her thing, but it didn't mean it was everyone else's. Increasingly she was noticing a trend for brides wanting a more over-the-top style for their special days.

Well, if that's what they want, then that's what I'll do.

She'd brought her business back from the brink of destruction—and her heart—and no way would she allow it to fall back down again. A few more top-notch clients would see her cemented as one of the premier bridal salon's in New York, a dream she'd been holding on to since her own personal happily-ever-after had shattered to smithereens.

Giving a sharp nod, she decisively walked up to the front, unlocking the ornate powder blue door and pushing it inwards, the tinkle from the doorbell filling her with a sense of satisfaction.

This was her home, her life, and her cheerful place.

Locking the door behind her, she moved through the front showroom to the back where her design room, fitting studio and living quarters were. It was small, and the Tribeca location hadn't come cheap but was worth every penny for the clientele it brought in.

Pushing open the interconnecting door from her

workroom—or design hub, as her friends referred to it —a short bark greeted her and two paws pressed against her legs.

"Smooch," she giggled. "Down. I'll walk you later, boy."

She dumped her cream leather tote bag onto the counter, popping her keys and now almost empty coffee cup beside it. Crouching, she indulged in a puppy snuggle with her miniature-sized King Charles Cavalier.

"At least I've got you. Who needs any other man?"

Maybe she should talk to her mother about her getting a dog. Smooch was the perfect male companion in Bekka's opinion and not once had he ever disappointed her. Maybe her mother would settle down on the revolving door of supposed 'true loves' if she had a dog to entertain.

Enough postulating about Mom, Bekka, it's time to work.

There were sketches to complete for her next collection, and fabric selections to finish. She was almost there, ahead of schedule, which made her feel better about the photo shoot she had booked for later that day. One which she was having to step in as the model for. Clara had canceled last minute yesterday. A friend who was also a model, her voice so croaky Bekka had struggled to make out the words. With no time to find another option, Bekka had decided to just model the dresses herself. Not the best solution, but at least she had a suitably sized slim figure, if not the height.

Walking out of the kitchen, she pulled the door closed, trying to ignore the doggy sigh that movement elicited. Her heels clicked loudly into the silence against the oak floorboards of her office. Pulling out her diary she triple checked there were no appointments other than the shoot until much later that afternoon, then got to work. It didn't take long to lose herself in a world of swirling skirts and whimsical details.

This collection she'd titled 'fairy-tale princess', at least in her mind. She'd decided the showstopper would be an ode to Cinderella, in the palest shade of duck egg blue. Voluminous skirts that glittered and shimmered at the slightest move. The backless style would require a lot of structure within the front and she pulled out a few swatches of interfacing from her book, checking her computer to see what fabric she still had in stock and what materials she'd need to place orders on.

Her shop was appointment only, though sometimes there would be knocks at the door with walk-ins. Unfortunately, it meant she worked mostly in silence, only the sounds of her pencils scratching against the parchment or her fingers tapping at her keyboard to keep her company. She loved mornings like this though, where she could lose herself in her work, and put onto paper the designs that chewed at her subconscious until she plucked them out, giving them freedom.

The phone buzzed, the interruption bringing with it a few quick barks. Connecting the call, she walked over to the door that connected to her living quarters and peered through the glass. Smooch sat on the other side, giving her a forlorn begging look, which Bekka rolled her eyes at.

"Hello, Something Blue Designs, Bekka Arden speaking."

There was a slight pause on the other end before a deep male voice cleared his throat. "Bekka. It's been a while."

Oh. She knew that voice.

"Noah Fox, as I live and breathe. How are you?" She asked, her tone dry.

"Great. Yourself?"

"Fine."

"Just fine?"

"Yes, Noah. I'm *just* fine. Five years is a long time since we last spoke. Did you call for idle chitchat? It's just I have a business to run. My 'little designer fun' I believe you once called it."

A soft chuckle came down the line, causing Bekka's stomach to tighten further. Noah Fox made her want to snarl just by breathing.

"Don't get your panties in a twist. Your bridal dress business is why I'm calling."

"Oh. My. Gosh. Do *not* tell me someone has agreed

to marry you? Has some woman actually captured that stony heart of yours?"

"No. My stony heart is perfectly safe, but thank you for your shocked concern. My sister, Valerie, has just become engaged and I may have mentioned your business to her. She's very interested in making an appointment. I thought since we were old friends, I'd make the call."

Bekka swallowed back the retort that sat on her tongue. She and Noah might have a long history of bickering and her dislike of him ran deep, but she couldn't knock back a client. Particularly his sister. She wouldn't admit it freely, but she wasn't obtuse with knowing just what Noah Fox was up to, and his famous Australian family. She'd seen the announcement for his sister's engagement to billionaire finance wizard Arnold Hemming on page six, the upcoming wedding named one of *the* weddings to be seen at. If she could snag Valerie Fox as her client, the last doubt surrounding her business would be gone.

"You've gone silent," Noah remarked, an odd tone she couldn't place in his voice.

"Sorry, busy morning. I'd absolutely love to have Valerie come in! Please pass on my congratulations to her. When suits the lucky bride to be? Or would she prefer I call her to arrange a time?"

Again with the soft chuckle. Bekka really wished he'd stop that. It didn't seem fair that a man who frustrated her to high blood pressure levels could also bring her insides undone with the sound of that laugh. After five years of not hearing it, she'd kind of hoped that reaction would have dissipated.

"How's this afternoon?"

Her heart skipped, and she rubbed at her chest area. "*This* afternoon?" Attempting to slow the rapid increase in her breathing, she snatched up her appointment book, flicking back to the page she'd only just looked at, already knowing that she had a reasonably full late afternoon. Straight after lunch, she'd left free on purpose in case the shoot went into overtime, but after that it was chaotic. "Um, I can do early afternoon." She squeaked, half hoping and praying that wouldn't work but also desperate to not lose Valerie as a potential bride.

She could hear Noah's muffled tone through the receiver and realized he was conferring with someone. It wasn't long before his voice came through again. "We can make that work. Can we take you to lunch first?"

Bekka's brows rose at the lovely offer. "I'd love to, but I'm afraid I'll be working."

"You know what they say… all work and no play makes Bekka a lonely gal."

"I don't think they say that. It must be an Australian thing." She replied with a snap. "Besides, like you can talk. You hightailed it out of New York City to return to work before the ink had even dried on your degree. If that saying applies to anyone, it's you."

She could hear the smile in his voice. Like warm

melted chocolate on a wintry day. Sickening, but addictive. And oh, so bad for you. "Touché. We'll see you at two p.m.?"

"Looking forward to it." Ignoring the plural term he'd used, she hung up. It wasn't like Noah Fox would actually come to her bridal studio with his sister. I mean, that was a job for mothers or bridesmaids. Not annoying brothers of the bride.

At least she hoped that would be the case.

Gulping down her last mouthful of now lukewarm coffee, she tossed her disposable cup into her wastebasket, wincing at the number of disposable cups already in there.

A morning's work later, Bekka stepped into one of her own gowns. The French guipure lace had cost a small fortune but was worth it for the quality. Slipping it up to sit just off her shoulders, the lace hugging her slim arms; she had her friend Chelsea do up the remaining buttons at the back.

This was the last of the designs to shoot, and one of her favorites from the collection. The mermaid tail skirt with tulle underlays gave her the allure of a stunning curvy shape. Her hair had been pulled into a loose braid by the hairstylist, but after two hours of photography, wisps had made their escape, dancing about her face.

She stepped in front of the mirror, its Hamptons white border was carved with a floral design that had spoken wedding studio to her, loud and clear. The image reflected at her made her smile at the same time as it made her stomach sink. This was a reworked version of her own wedding dress. The one she'd never ended up putting on.

The wedding that had never happened.

She grimaced at the sadness in her eyes. *Pull it together, Bekka. No one wants an image of a sad bride.* Her rose petal pink lips stretched, her white teeth gleaming through the smile that almost appeared genuine. She placed the dainty tiara at the center of her crown; the comb slotting through her hair to nestle into place. The whisper of a fine tulle veil floated down her back, trailing across the ground at her feet.

"Honestly Bekka, you make *the* most beautiful bride ever. Whatever was Connor thinking?" Chelsea's southern drawl scratched at her thoughts.

Bekka swallowed, thrown at Chelsea's comment, which ran so close to her own thoughts. She didn't want to meander any further down the memory path of her ill-fated engagement to Connor Chivers.

"Thank you, that's kind of you to say. Could you pull the front veil over, please? I think I'd like some shots with it in place. Maybe sitting over by the window?"

"Absolutely. But can we do a few in front of the mirror here first? It's perfectly framed and we get that stunning back of the dress, that heart-shape cut into the silk mesh is just so romantic."

Bekka shrugged, happy to defer to Chelsea's professional take.

Chelsea had brought along music, insisting it helped her create the right mood for her photos. Bekka's mouth twitched as the latest pop sensation came on. Words of love filled the air with a cutesy beat that had Bekka's hips swaying unconsciously, the shutter of Chelsea's camera creating its own accompanying beat. Closing her eyes, she swirled, her arm catching in the train of her veil, her lips pulled into a soft smile. So lost in the moment, it took her a minute to realize the music was switched off, replaced by silence.

Her eyes fluttered open. She faced the mirror, her reflection not the only image staring back at her. In the background stood a very familiar man, whose green eyes found hers with an eerie sense of ease. Had she ever seen Noah Fox look shell-shocked?

Spinning around, she plastered a smile into place. "I'm so sorry. We must have lost track of the time." Reaching up, she plucked out the comb, ducking out from underneath the yards of tulle attached to it and handed it to Chelsea's outstretched arm, mouthing a silent thank you. Marching forward she placed a hand out towards the woman who stood beside Noah.

"You must be Valerie Fox? It's such a pleasure to meet you, I'm Bekka Arden."

She congratulated herself on the level tone of her voice, impressed it hadn't wobbled. She certainly felt all sorts of wobbly inside.

"That I am, and can I just say that dress you're in is insanely beautiful. You do your own modeling?"

Bekka felt a satisfying warmth spread through her at Valerie's praise. "Not normally, my model had to cancel at the last minute."

"You certainly look the part." Noah's voice was soft, with an odd tinge.

She gritted her teeth, and by some miracle kept a smile on her face. Her eyes flicked to his, not expecting the heat that had deepened them to more of a bottle green, rather than emerald. Years might have passed, but it seemed Noah Fox was still incredibly handsome, and still incredibly annoying.

"Yes, well." She didn't finish the sentence. He knew well that she wouldn't be a bride anytime soon. His best friend had shattered those dreams three days before she'd been meant to walk down the aisle. Her wedding, that she'd spent a lifetime dreaming of, had been demolished with a few short words. "If you wouldn't mind giving me a minute to change and then we can get started. If you'd like to have a look around the studio, please do so. I'm just completing my latest collection so I'm also more than happy to show you those sketches or we can work on a couture designed piece depending on your timelines."

"My goodness. Noah said you were the best around,

and he wasn't lying. From what I can see, it all looks exquisite. How on earth will I choose?"

"You'll know it when you see it." She remarked with a smile, as the other woman wandered towards the racks. Bekka threw Noah a small frown. He'd said *she* was the best around? That didn't sound like him at all. Not that she uttered those words. She'd had enough mountains to climb back to her current position. As far as she was concerned, whatever the bride wanted, she'd get. And Bekka would make sure it was the best dress she could make happen.

Excusing herself and avoiding his eyes, she walked over to Chelsea who was packing up her gear.

"Sorry about this, did you get enough shots of this dress?"

"Oh, hon. You just wait—I got the most perfect shot of you twirling in the mirror, looking every bit the besotted woman in love about to marry the man of her dreams. Speaking of… Who's the eye candy? Not the groom I imagine!"

"No, that's the brother." She said flatly.

"You two know each other?" Chelsea raised her brows, most likely in response to what Bekka wasn't saying.

"We did. Once. He's Connor's best friend. I have to go change, make sure you leave your invoice on my desk."

"Okay. I can see now isn't the time, but tonight. You need to spill. Everything!"

Bekka offered a tight nod before she sashayed out of the room. Tonight she was meeting the No Brides Club girls, and since she'd invited Chelsea personally to join the club, she knew she wouldn't get out of going tonight without a solid explanation. The members were all successful, career savvy and gorgeous women, inside and out, and every one of them knew of her past with Connor. The man who'd single-handedly ruined her hopes, dreams, and almost her career in one day.

A message he delivered through his best friend, Noah Fox.

Noah might be all types of eye candy, but he was also off-limits and the last person she wanted to see.

CHAPTER 2

*N*oah tried to level out his breathing that had skyrocketed to the point he wondered at his health. Bekka Arden was every bit as beautiful as he'd remembered. Unfortunately, it seemed she also hadn't lost her dislike of him.

Seeing her twirling in the mirror just now, he thought his heart would erupt.

Her face had been relaxed, a soft smile of warmth and euphoria gracing her features. She could stop men in their tracks with her classic features and piercing brown eyes, but in that dress… wow.

Connor might have decided he and Bekka weren't right for each other, a decision Noah had urged him to consider very carefully, but it seemed Noah was still in the doghouse over that in Bekka's eyes.

"Noah, come look at this."

He took a few steps further into the studio. He

hadn't planned to play much of a part in this activity, but after he'd made the call and heard Bekka's sweet tone over the phone, he hadn't been able to stop himself from tagging along.

Valerie held out the skirts of a dress that appeared to be wider than his car. "Um. Pretty. Bit big though, isn't it? Will you be able to walk or dance in it?"

"Ever the practical one. But ok, you might have a point."

His sister continued to walk along, her fingers trailing along the hangers. He could tell from her rapt expression that she would find something from Bekka's collection.

The woman of his thoughts reappeared, the click of her heels against the floorboards signaling her presence. She wore slim-fitting jeans, a crisp white blouse with a soft pink jacket over the top. Very elegant and demure.

"Sorry again about the delay." She said with a welcoming smile. He noted she appeared to be avoiding his eyes, but he wasn't having that.

"Bekka, it's been a long time. The place looks amazing. Very deserving of your talents."

She gaped at him, her wide eyes blinking like he'd just suggested she dance the macarena.

"Thank you." She murmured stiltedly. Her brows pulled together before smoothing back into the polite expression she'd held when she'd walked out.

"This is my most recent couture collection. Every

design you see is still available and will be created exclusively for you and custom fitted by myself. The collection on the far side is the lower-priced ones. There are a few designs towards the end of the rack which are sample only so if you like those we would have to fit that exact dress, but I offer them at a discount since they are the end of that line." She pulled out a cream notebook. The solo word 'dreams' was inscribed in gold lettering across the top. "I've also brought out my sketchbook. I don't normally offer this to clients, but I'm going to be cheeky and admit I read all about your engagement on page six. Would I be correct in assuming you're after something that's more, one-of-a-kind?"

"You've read me like a book," Valerie replied with a wink. "I honestly don't even know where to start!"

"In that case, shall we take a seat? I can offer you tea, coffee, or a glass of champagne, perhaps? There's a comfortable lounge in the fitting room where we could sit and discuss some ideas. Then if you'd like to try on some styles, you can get an idea of what shapes are best suited to your figure and what's most comfortable. Some brides love the big Cinderella style dresses but they also want to party like its nineteen ninety-nine which is just impossible to do with all those layers."

Valerie chewed her lip a little. "Noah just said almost the same thing. I do love the over-the-top ball-gown style, the full princess look, but my fiancé and I are taking dance lessons." She leaned in to whisper conspiratorially. "We want to organize one of those wedding party dances."

Noah held in a groan, especially when Bekka's eyes lit with interest. Valerie had already mentioned her idea to him. He hadn't had the heart to outright refuse her, though he hadn't given up hope that she'd change her mind. Dancing solo with a beautiful woman? Sign him up. Dancing a group choreography in top hat and tails? Not a chance.

His sister really had some bizarre ideas.

Bekka grinned. "That sounds like such fun. Are you part of the wedding party, Noah?"

Her eyes sparkled with a wicked humor that reminded him of the first day they'd met. The day he'd fallen for Bekka only to find out she was well and truly taken.

"Yep." He quipped, his smile tacked in place with sheer force of will.

"Well, that does sound like fun. I hope you're planning a videographer, Valerie? Those memories are ones for a lifetime of enjoyment and viewing. Maybe even YouTube?"

He could tell she was enjoying this.

"I believe you mentioned champagne?" He inserted, knowing the mention of a celebratory glass of bubbles would distract his sister.

"Of course. Come on through. Will you be joining us, Noah? Or I can highly recommend a coffee shop just around the corner from here."

It was clear from her hopeful expression just which option she'd prefer he take, but no way was he leaving here. The chance to spend time in her company was too alluring.

"Oh no, Noah's staying. He's my right-hand man for all of this wedding business! My mom can't fly at present and my best friend lives overseas so he's standing in. Do you mind if he takes photos of everything to share with my other cohorts? I hope that's not too much of an imposition."

Surprise shone in Bekka's caramel coffee eyes. "Oh." Her mouth rounded in a perfect O shape, the pale pink lipstick highlighting her lips. She recovered quickly. "No, of course not. Is your mom okay?"

Noah ushered a hand at Valerie's back, escorting her after Bekka, who led the way out of the front showroom into a room at the back. He had to hand it to Bekka. The style of her shop spoke of the utmost elegance and supreme quality. And every inch reminded him of her.

"She broke her ankle, playing soccer with the nephews," Noah replied, realizing Valerie was distracted and in bridal world, not at all following the conversation.

"Oh, my goodness. I hope she's okay?" Genuine concern shone on Bekka's face.

"She'll recover. It's a friendly reminder for her to slow down a little. Neither of my parents appears to understand the concept."

"Family trait." She muttered under her breath, but Noah caught every word, chuckling in amusement.

"How about you ladies sit and Bekka you can direct me to the champagne. I think I'm more useful in that area."

Uncertainty crossed her face, and she flicked her gaze between the two before pulling her lip up into a half grimace. "I keep the supplies in my kitchen. It's a lovely offer, but I should probably go—"

Valerie interrupted, holding a commanding hand up to stop Bekka's words, and then patted Noah on the chest. "Nonsense. Noah's domesticated enough to sort that out for us. I know your time's limited, Bekka, and I cannot *wait* to see your new designs."

Noah offered Bekka a conspiratorial smile and walked out of the room in the direction she'd pointed, moving further down the corridor where he could see a door. High pitched yapping greeted him the minute his hand touched the doorknob. Instead of deterring him, he pushed the door inwards, and was enveloped by two things that hit him at once. One, a tiny ball of caramel, brown and white fur with ears that appeared too big for it, and eyes that searched his soul with their little pleading orbs; two, Bekka's perfume. It hadn't been as apparent within her shop, perhaps because there'd been a stream of other smells to dilute it. But right within the entrance to her personal abode, it engulfed him. Gardenias and a hint of cinnamon. It was a scent he'd never been able to forget.

Smiling a wry smile to no one in particular, he kneeled to greet the little puffball who had sat obediently at his polished shoes. "Who might you be?" he asked and was immediately rewarded with the puppy's belly to scratch. He happily obliged.

"You've met Smooch, I see." Bekka's voice had him glancing over his shoulder.

"You called your dog, Smooch?"

"It's a long story."

"I'd like to hear it." He continued to rub the soft belly, feeling a slight lick at his hand when he briefly paused his administrations. "Cute dog, regardless of the name." He smirked.

"Kitchen's straight ahead and to the right, you can't miss it. Champagne will be in the fridge and glasses are already on the counter. Thank you," she paused, "for offering to help."

He stood, straightening his tall frame, which towered a little over hers. In heels, she gained a few inches.

"You sound surprised."

"I am," she replied with a clipped tone. With that, she spun and walked back down the hallway. He pretended he didn't watch her go. Glancing back down at the dog—whom he couldn't bring himself to call Smooch—it gifted him a forlorn puppy expression that almost appeared to be relaying his thoughts to perfection; *You've got it bad, man.*

Bekka swallowed back an odd nervousness as she returned to the fitting room. Valerie was pouring over her designs, her quiet exclaims of delight a good sign that she approved of what she was seeing. Bekka mentally crossed her fingers. She knew she was a talented designer, and took the time to ensure that the bride was always one hundred percent happy whenever they purchased from her label, but earning Valerie's approval seemed more important than all of that.

The addition of having Noah around was more unsettling than she'd expected. As was his attitude towards her. He'd changed in the five years since they'd been in the same room. Not that their last conversation had been in any way pleasant.

He might have just been trying to help, but in doing so he'd crushed their friendship, and her relationship with Connor.

"Bekka, these are just divine. I want to choose them all!" exclaimed Valerie.

Bekka laughed. "Well, I guess you could do hourly changes, though I imagine you'd end up feeling rather exhausted. How about you tell me a little more about what you envision for your wedding? Do you have a theme? Have you hired a planner or are you going it solo?"

"I've hired a wedding planner. Emilia Sullivan of

Happy Ever After weddings, actually I messaged her saying I was coming to check out your designs, and she sent back an enthusiastic response stating you were her top suggestion. You come highly recommended."

Bekka ignored the enquiring gleam in Valerie's eyes. "Emilia's a good friend. You're in wonderful hands with her. As it happens, she would have been my top pick too had you not decided yet on a wedding planner."

"You guys are so lucky, the wedding industry must be so much fun," Valerie remarked.

"It is." Bekka smiled, choosing not to outline how tough it had been to crack into and that it had taken hours of blood, sweat, and tears to reach this stage. And a hefty loan and tremendous gamble. But it seemed to pay off for now. Designing Valerie Fox's wedding dress would be the cherry on top of the cake.

"So I'm going for a sort of whimsical yet classically elegant princess theme. Loads of fairy lights, all shades of white. The men will wear black tux and tails, with a white vest, bow tie, and top hat. All the flowers will be white with ivy for greenery. I'm getting topiary white roses installed everywhere and an arch to stand under for the ceremony. I guess I want my dress to be that ultimate princess style. But also practical. Is that even possible? Am I making any sense?" The younger woman let out a bark of laughter, as though she knew she was reaching for the stars, standing only on a short ladder.

"We'll make it possible. I saw you eyeing one design out in the front with the yards of skirts. We could do something like that but have the skirt detachable? So, for the reception, it could become something lighter and more manageable for your flash mob idea."

"Really? OH! That would be just perfect!"

"What would be perfect?" Noah's voice interrupted.

Bekka shifted, glancing over to the doorway, her jaw dropping in surprise. Smooch was cocooned within the crook of Noah's arm, his enormous hands cradling three sparkling glasses of champagne.

She shook off her confusion, jumping up to assist. "Let me help you with that."

A slight tinge of red flushed his cheeks. "Sorry about your dog. He kept skittering between my feet to the point I worried I'd step on him, so I just scooped him up. It seemed to be what he wanted."

Bekka swallowed, unable to form any coherent response. Smooch had *never* shown any preference for another person, certainly not a man. He barely tolerated Bekka's friends when they came to visit, which is why she locked him in her living abode whenever she had customers. Seemed Noah was the exception to that rule.

"He's not usually a people person. You must have the knack." She hadn't meant to sound so disbelieving, but Noah's slight brow raise told her she'd missed the mark.

Reaching out, Bekka took two of the glasses from

his hands, the slight brush of his fingers against hers giving her tummy another odd wobble. What was with her today? She handed Valerie a glass, and then cradled her own, raising a toast to the bride to be. She wouldn't normally have a drink with clients, but it seemed rude not to take at least a sip after Noah had poured her a glass.

"That is the cutest dog ever!" Valerie pronounced after taking a deep gulp from her glass. Bekka was realizing that Valerie spoke in exclamation marks more often than not.

"He's called Smooch," Noah smirked.

"Oh em gee! That's even sweeter! Oh, can you imagine if we got mom to bring out one of the new litter for the wedding? It could be the ring bearer!"

Bekka caught Noah's grimace, though whether that was at his sister's suggestion or her high pitched enthusiastic tone, she couldn't tell.

"Valerie, I'm not sure Mom will want to arrange for a puppy to fly to America for your wedding. Maybe if you'd gone with their suggestion to have the wedding back home in Australia."

"Oh, don't you start. Arnold's work is so busy right now. Besides, he's offered to pay for all the flights so we can have it here in New York. His granny is eighty-nine. She's refusing to fly and quite frankly going against her wishes scares me more than the lineup outside Saks during Black Friday Sales."

"Well, if you're set on having a dog, perhaps Bekka

can loan us this little guy. You'll be coming to the wedding, won't you?" Noah's eyes pinned her to the spot, leaving her devoid of normal function. Attend the wedding? *Was he crazy?*

"I, uh, well." *Nice one, Bekka. Really showing that customer service and high functioning ability right now.*

Valerie stepped into her personal space and threw her arms around her, the hug showering her in a cloud of Chanel No. Five. "No pressure, but of course, you have to be there!"

Guess that answered that. She knew her smile lacked support, the slack feeling was probably apparent across her entire face.

"So. Now that's settled. Can we try on some dresses? Also, do you think we can get a matching silk bow tie for Smooch? To match Arnolds? He's okay with guests, right? The guest list is blossoming with every phone call my mom makes." Valerie rolled her eyes, thankfully not noticing the three shades paler Bekka went.

A soft, warm hand met the small of her back. "I'll talk to her." Noah murmured at her ear.

His words shouldn't have calmed her instantly, yet they did. She threw him a soft smile, his answering hers instantly. Even with their differences, Noah had always had an uncanny ability to read her like an open book.

Stowing away all these odd thoughts and feelings to decipher another time, she turned back to Valerie. "I'm sure we can arrange for a bow tie for Smooch, though I should warn you he's not normally much of a people person. He might be okay so long as I'm close, though I've never taken him to a wedding. And yes, let's try on some dresses."

Taking a well-needed sip of her champagne, she walked over and placed the glass on the sill, then left the room to select some gowns that showcased the various dress shapes for Valerie to choose from. She ignored the cool air that rushed in to replace Noah's handprint. She already had a powerful image in her mind of a bridal gown that fit Valerie's descriptions perfectly. Layers of tulle, silk, lace, and Swarovski seed beads. Intricate embroidery and beading on the under layer. The top layers of skirts a separate piece. Unfortunately, she had a jam-packed afternoon, and tonight was her standing evening catch-up with her other friends from the No Brides Club, but perhaps after that, she could dedicate some time to sketches and fabric selections.

The thought left her grinning and giddy with happiness.

CHAPTER 3

Bekka was late, as usual, her friends already in their preferred spot within the dining room at the Briarwood Tavern. They were chatting amongst themselves, waiting for her arrival before ordering anything.

"Sorry, sorry, sorry." She said with a grimace, leaning down to greet Marnie, who was closest. She proceeded around the table, dolling out hugs and cheek kisses.

Their group was growing again, and her heart gave a warm shimmy of happiness and strength to be surrounded by such an amazing group of friends. She'd met Devon when the pretty blonde with the southern belle accent had come in to collect her wedding dress ordered by her sister, Marnie. Devon had the dress but no fiancé, having been unceremoniously dumped before her wedding just like Bekka herself. The two had hit it off on that common ground and had been firm friends since. Devon was now headfirst in love with Sven, a vet and TV host. Quite a few of the others had all also found their true loves and flung off the No Brides Club mantra, but thankfully it hadn't stopped them coming along.

Bekka knew without this crew she never would have taken the plunge and invested in her Tribeca location, which was already paying off, her business financials in a far superior position to where they'd been this time last year.

"A little birdy informed me you've snagged the contract for this season's must-see wedding, designing Valerie Fox's dress. Congratulations, lovely!"

"Thanks, Emilia. Actually, that's why I'm running late. My last client's fitting ran early, so I used the time to start sketching ideas for Valerie's dress."

"And lost track of time?" Devon drawled with a grin.

Bekka held her palms up and grinned back. "Guilty. I cannot wait to get started on this dress. It will be just beautiful."

"Oh hon, every dress you make is beautiful. You work so hard. This will be the well-deserved last kick required to put everything else behind you. Maybe even take a step back and take a breath." They all knew how much this business meant to her.

"Enough about that," Bekka said, feeling heat behind her eyes and not wanting to get all emotional at the clear support that shone back in front of her. "Who needs a drink? It must be my treat."

"Not so fast, lady." Chelsea stood, joining Bekka before she could escape to the bar. Her friend continued in a whisper, "I still want the rest of the story about this Noah."

"There's not much to tell. We met at college. He and Connor really hit it off as friends."

"And…"

Bekka rolled her eyes. "And… Noah and I didn't hit it off so well. In fact, we usually only conversed through needling bickering or insults but we tolerated each other for the sake of Connor. Then to top that all off, he was the one to deliver the good news that Connor wouldn't be turning up at our wedding."

Chelsea gasped. "You never mentioned that Connor didn't call off the wedding himself!"

Bekka swallowed. "It's not really something I like to talk about. It's downright humiliating. I date a guy since seventh grade, take my time to judge that he truly loves me and I finally let myself fall for him only to have him up and disappear. The whole situation, any memories of it, makes me feel ill. So I prefer not to re-hash ancient history."

"I assumed from the way Noah looked at you today that maybe you were once an item. He was practically devouring you with his eyes."

"What! That's nonsense."

"Suit yourself. But that's what I saw."

Bekka shrugged off the comments, choosing not to pay her friend's overactive imagination any heed. "Anyway, it's all water under the bridge. Connor is well in my past, as is Noah. I am grateful to him for thinking of me for his sister's wedding dress though."

"And so he should, you're the best!"

The rest of the evening was full of laughter and relaxation amongst good friends, leaving Bekka feeling refreshed. Arriving home later than planned, a few joyous barks greeted her from Smooch, who followed at her heels as she undressed and got ready for bed. The little puppy wasn't the biggest fan of her standing Thursday night tradition, but at least they'd come to an understanding of sorts. Bekka would be out for the evening, but once home, Smooch got her full attention. After a quick trip outside for Smooch to do his doggy thing, Bekka locked up and fell into bed, expecting sleep to claim her instantly.

Instead, she tossed and turned, earning a few quick barks from her companion.

Noah Fox re-entering her life had thrown her for a loop. Not that he was really re-entering her life. But he was here, in town, and after today's fitting, his sister was now a client. Did that mean she'd be seeing more of him? And his insistence she attend Valerie's wedding?

She hadn't seen or heard from Noah since three days before her own disastrous planned nuptials. When he served her the news that Connor had left town and couldn't go through with the wedding. Goodness, she'd been a wreck. And she'd taken it out on Noah. Connor hadn't even had the guts to come speak to her himself, sending his best friend to do his dirty work. That had never sat well with Bekka, though now with perspective she could see that perhaps Connor had been right. They hadn't been right for each other and had been heading in different directions. But it still hurt to think of the humiliation.

She'd only just launched her label, had been working out of her home, and had built up a few clients. One of her dresses had featured in Vogue's bridal issue and she'd been on cloud nine planning her own wedding to Connor.

Except that was just it. It had been *her* wedding and only hers. Connor hadn't been around. He had been working long hours, and every time she'd tried to talk to him about the wedding, he'd put the decisions back to her. His disinterest should have been a glaring neon sign, but wrapped up in her own world, she'd totally missed it.

Stop it, Bekka. Torturing yourself with memories doesn't help anyone. It's behind you now. Time to look forward and only forward.

If only mentally ordering herself to do so made it that easy.

A few days later, Noah strolled along the edge of Central Park, trying to formulate another excuse to go visit Bekka.

He liked New York City. The energy, the buzz, the opportunities that could almost be smelled in the air as strongly as car fumes. But he didn't miss it, not like he missed home. He missed the feeling of being able to drink in fresh air and walk without tumbling over a million people. It was nice knowing at least someone. His parents' hotel chain chose locations that were premium, but also exclusive. Their bookings were for those wanting to escape the hustle and bustle and really reconnect with their partners. Enjoy life's finest.

His suggestion to expand into America hadn't been met with enthusiasm, but Noah knew in his gut that it could take the business to that next level. Plus, it had given him the opportunity to come back here, to deal with some unresolved feelings that he'd hoped would eventually go away but had yet to do so.

Bekka Arden had been the first person he'd met at Columbia, and he'd fallen like a ton of bricks. That had been until she'd introduced her long-time, childhood sweetheart, Connor. He'd figured with time the unrequited feelings would just disperse. There were plenty more fish in the sea, right? Except they hadn't. With every date, every woman who had passed in and out of his life, he'd compared them to her. To Bekka.

Not once had any lived up to the expectations.

His phone beeped, showing an incoming call. Seeing Valerie's number, he answered straight away.

"Hey, sis. Aren't you meant to be knee-deep in wedding planning?"

"Yes, that's why I'm calling. Arnold has to fly to San Francisco tonight and well... We've hardly seen each other, so I've decided to go too."

Noah frowned, unsure exactly where Valerie was going with this. "Okay. Do you need me to water your flowers or something?"

"Actually yes, please, that would be amazing. My cleaner always drowns them, so I'll ask her not to this time."

"That doesn't sound like the real reason you called." Noah gave a lopsided grin to no one in particular. His sister was always like this, doing seven things at once but never really *doing* any of them properly.

"Right. I need you to take a few appointments for me."

Ominous silence followed her sentence. Noah side-stepped out of the steady flow of foot traffic and moved to lean against the outer fence that circled the park. "Uh, what sort of appointments, exactly?"

"Nothing bad! It's just I'm so swamped with work and all this wedding planning. There's just *so* much to do!"

He didn't bother to point out it had been her idea to push for a quick wedding so they could get the venue they wanted, or how she'd had to have *the* wedding of the season, complete with a horse-drawn Cinderella-style carriage, ice sculptures of the happy couple (during the height of summer) and a guest list that rivaled the crowd at a home team finals game. He sucked in a quick breath, then expelled it through his nose. "All right. Just what do you need me to do?"

"Uh well." She paused as though consulting a list. A click that sounded suspiciously like a clipboard sounded through the phone. "I need linens selected, but you grew up in the same household as I did so I doubt you'll struggle there, just make sure they are all white. Check-in with the florist to view some mock-ups—though so long as they are white and smell good, I'm happy. The ice artist has done some computer mock-ups, if you could swing by and just check there's nothing out of the ordinary there. Did you get that funny post I forwarded? Could you imagine if something like that happened! I'd die."

Noah shook his head gently, used to his sister's erratic ways of conversation.

"Oh, and I need you to collect samples from Bekka. She just texted me a sketch. It. Is. To. Die. For! Seriously, how do you even know her?"

At Valerie's mention of Bekka's name, his concentration kicked back in full force. A visit to Bekka's studio and another chance to see her was high on his list. He'd been trying to think of an excuse to casually drop past, so this seemed serendipitous.

"Noah?"

"Yep?"

"Were you listening?"

"Of course. Linens, flowers, ice sculpture minus any random appendages, and visit Bekka. Theme is white."

"Smarty pants. I also asked you how you know Bekka, but I have to dash so I'll let you fill me in on that another time. Either way, I owe you big time!"

"Don't take this the wrong way, but aren't many of these things jobs that you could ask your wedding planner to do? I mean, isn't that what you're paying her for?"

There was a small huff, followed by a sigh. "I guess, yes, but these are such small things. Besides, I thought you came out to help me with the wedding? That you wanted to spend some time in New York, reconnecting with friends and getting to know Arnold and hanging out with me. Please, Noah?"

He chuckled. "I'll do them. I just thought I'd mention it in case you'd forgotten you had, in fact, hired a planner."

"You really think you're funny, but you're not," Valerie said with dramatic resignation to her tone.

"Maybe you can just email me a copy of your spreadsheet or whatever you just read off."

"I thought you'd never ask. Actually, before I go, there's a cake tasting at nine tomorrow morning. You *cannot* miss it. Emilia pulled every string in the book to get me a booking with this guy. He's a cake genius. Like masterful. Cake to transport you to heaven, all packaged in exquisite elegance."

"Surely you want to choose your own cake?" His brows shot up, his tone incredulous.

"Nope. You're the cake expert in our family. I'm happy to leave that one entirely in your hands, so long as—"

"Let me guess… so long as it's white?"

"Bingo. I'll text you the list. I love you! Best brother ever."

"Yeah, yeah. Love you too." He hung up, knowing a cheesy grin spread across his face. Erratic she might be in her chatter, but in her mind, she knew exactly how she wanted this wedding to look.

Big plus for him. Now he got to go cake tasting and had an excuse to see Bekka again. All he had to do was talk Bekka into coming along with him to taste cake so he could start smoothing out the past that still sat like a wedge between them. Then he could work out if these feelings that still dogged him were the real deal or just guilt-colored glasses.

Holding his arm out, he flagged down a cab, the sunshine yellow easy to spot in the traffic. No time like the present to get started.

Noah's taxi pulled up at the curb outside Something Blue Designs. He handed over a few bills, waving off the change, before stepping out and walking up the front path. Bekka was crouched in the glass window display, her tight black dress outlining her slim figure to perfection. If that was her marketing strategy for getting noticed he had to give her points for creativity.

The door jingled as he stepped through, tapering off as smooth and soulful jazz replaced the noise. No words, just a pleasant background fuzz to stop the space feeling empty.

"I'll be right with you," Bekka sang out.

"No rush," Noah replied, catching the faint harrumph that followed his words. "Just me."

"Twice in the space of a week. To what do I owe the pleasure this time?" she stepped out of the window. Strands of her deep melted chocolate colored hair had escaped and tangled about her face. She blew a few strands away before huffing as they returned to the exact same spot. She hooked them behind her ears with economical movements, very similar to how she'd used to do when bored during lectures or in study groups. Bekka hadn't been a very interested business student, even though she'd had the brains.

"I'm here on behalf of Valerie. But before I launch into that, what CD is this?"

She pursed her lips, tapping a polished fingernail against her cheek before snapping her fingers. "Smooth Jazz. I can find you the cover."

"It's a disc?" he said with surprise.

"Yep. I'm one of those old school people who are yet

to make the leap to a music subscription. I have about ten or so I just rotate. I don't exactly need the latest hits playing. I'm creating mood, not a dance class." Her smile was impish.

"I like it. It's perfect for mood music. I've been searching for something just like it."

"Oh?" She beckoned for him to follow her, flicking the front door lock over before she led him out to her design room and rifled through some overflowing drawers before coming up with a royal blue case and handing it to him.

"Dad's been looking for mood music for our piano room at the Sorrento location." He glanced down, his eyes doing a quick scan of the titles before he turned it over and snapped a picture of the cover. "You look like you need an assistant." He flicked a finger about the space which was packed with rolls of fabric, files that were overflowing with paper, and tilting piles of books.

Bekka turned, taking in the entire space. The corner of her mouth pulled to the side before she sighed. "Probably. Believe it or not, I know where everything is in this chaos. Maybe next year."

"Surely your finances are in good shape? You've had a steady stream of biggish name clients this past year."

She spun back to him, a frown marring her otherwise perfect face. "How do you know anything about my client list?"

"I read the papers. Don't change the subject. If you need someone to look over your books, I'm happy to help. Though your grades were better than mine, so I can't imagine you're doing anything but a stellar job of running your business."

She scrunched her nose, then cocked her head to one side. "Thank you. I think. My business is in good shape. I just want to wait before putting any strain on it, that's all."

An odd look passed over her features. If pushed he'd say it was concern. She went to step around him, but he placed an arm at her wrist, stilling her movements. "Bekka? What's wrong?"

"Nothing." She blurted.

"It's not nothing." He quipped back, pinning her with his gaze.

A small sound of frustration erupted from her lips. "What are you even doing here? My business is fine, thanks to you, and I'm planning for it to stay that way. I don't need your interference."

"I'm not interfering, I'm offering help, from one successful business owner to another. And what do you mean 'thanks to me'?"

She curled her hand away, massaging the spot before crossing her arms across her chest. "I don't really want to get into this right now. I've got work to do."

An ache formed around his heart. Whatever she wasn't telling him, it seemed big, and his stomach dropped, sensing it wasn't good. "Let me take you out for dinner tonight, and you can tell me then?"

Her lips thinned. "Why are you prolonging this? Noah, I appreciate you bringing your sister to me as a client but honestly don't you think our past has spoken for itself? My business flatlined after Connor called off the wedding. A decision he made thanks to you."

Noah reeled back as though someone had hit him. "Because of me? I didn't tell Connor to call off the wedding. I only delivered the message. Which, I'll add, I told him wasn't right, but he said he couldn't do it himself." Noah swallowed back the acid that burned his throat. He didn't want to throw his buddy under the bus, but nor did he want this misunderstanding of Bekka's continuing. She had the situation wrong. "Connor called me that morning, telling me he couldn't go through with the wedding. I told him he had to tell you in person. He said he couldn't. That if he saw you, he'd cave. He didn't want to hurt you and threatened to just walk away without speaking to you at all. That's why I came. I didn't want you left in the dark any longer than you needed to be. What made you think otherwise?"

"Connor. I saw him a month later, ran into him. I broke down in public and he said you'd talked him into calling it off. That you could see he and I weren't right for one another. He said you'd planted the seeds, and he hadn't been able to see anything since, that what we wanted in life was too different and we'd end up a divorce statistic in less than two years."

Silence followed her words. Noah could hear a

clock ticking behind the whisper of jazz music from the front room. His breathing was loud and slightly labored after Bekka's words. *Connor had said that?*

Pain and anguish flooded him, and an anger so intense that he thought he'd burst. He shook his head, his entire body heavy with the realization of how Bekka must have spent the past five years blaming him. No wonder she'd answered none of his attempts to reach out to her.

"I may have had a few doubts about how well-suited you and Connor were, but I never told him not to marry you. Goodness, Bekka, we were all friends. Connor became one of my best mates. I wanted you to be happy."

She bit her lip; the move leaving it ruby red. He noted her face only held minimal makeup. Not that she'd ever needed a lot with her clear as silk skin.

"My business folded after I called the wedding off. I lost all my clients. Some canceled after hearing my fiancé had walked away three days prior to our wedding. And then some I lost because I was a mess."

Her voice was tiny, and he did the only thing he could think of, folding her into his arms and holding her tight.

"I'm sorry." It was all he could think to say. It wasn't nearly enough, but only time could show Bekka the truth of his words.

CHAPTER 4

oah still held her within his embrace. She snuggled in, taking comfort from his arms. Had she ever realized how big he really was? He felt like a giant bear, and it was wonderful. Relief rushed through her at finally expelling the hurt that she'd held on to tight.

It had been five years. It was too long to still be holding a grudge. Besides, her business was solid now —or would be after Valerie's wedding—a client she owed to Noah. Connor's words from that day had never seemed to sit comfortably. In fact, his entire persona from that encounter had left her feeling odd and as though she'd never truly known the man he was.

What did that say about her? That she'd been so in love with the idea of having the big wedding and happily-ever-after that she hadn't stopped to consider the man she'd chosen to marry wasn't the right man at all? So much for her childhood promise to become nothing like her mother.

Sniffling slightly, she took a small step back. "Sorry," she let out a short laugh that fell a little flat, "I didn't mean to cry all over you."

"I'm not. I'm glad the air's been cleared a little. I always wondered why you'd gone so cold after the breakup and returned none of my calls. We were friends, Bekka. Good ones. Can't we be again?"

His voice held a pleading tone that melted some ice that clung to her heart. They may not have been best buddies, but Noah had always been there, and he'd always been honest to her. Sometimes brutally so, but it had been honesty she'd often needed to hear. Hindsight made her see that now.

"I think saying we were good friends might stretch the term, but I'm happy to set the past aside. Friends," she smiled, holding out a hand to shake. An odd tingle formed the moment his palm met hers and she frowned, pulling her hand away quickly. "You mentioned you had some things to discuss for Valerie?"

He cleared his throat a little. "Yes. I'm here to collect her sketches and fabric samples and also talk you into coming cake tasting with me."

Bekka's brow quirked in bemusement. "Cake tasting?"

Noah shrugged. "She's going with Arnold to San Francisco but the tasting's tomorrow morning and she can't let the opportunity slide."

"So she's sending you?"

"Well, I am the resident cake expert." He held his arms out and did a suave little turn, his expression smug.

Bekka giggled. Noah had always loved his cake. "I can't believe she's letting you choose the cake. Where is it? I'm really swamped right now with work…" her words trailed off as he shook his head at her.

"Don't be daft. Everyone can make time for cake. It's with Pierre Humbert."

Bekka's brows shot up, her voice squeaky. "The Pierre Humbert! He's booked out for years. How did Valerie swing that?"

"Her wedding planner, apparently."

"Actually, that makes sense. Emilia makes miracles happen." Bekka was in awe of the other woman.

"I'll pick you up at eight-thirty." Noah quipped, as though it were a done deal.

Bekka sighed. "As much as I'd love to, I wasn't kidding when I said I'm swamped. I just don't think I can." The words hurt to speak, and not only because Pierre's cakes were legendary and apparently as close to eating pure heaven as possible. She wanted to spend the time with Noah, to reconnect their old friendship, but at the same time, she felt strange doing so.

"All work and no play makes—"

"Yes, Bekka a bore, I know. I'm sure we had this same conversation recently?"

"We did. Which is why I'm not taking no for an

answer. Surely there are errands I can run for you to help free up your time." He looked about her space. "Can I install some cupboards for you, perhaps?"

She gave his arm a light whack. "Shouldn't you be working or something?"

"I've given myself a few days off. I have meetings and a few locations for visits next week, but those are secret, so shhhh. Officially, I'm here on holidays and to spend time with Valerie."

"You really are the perfect brother, aren't you?" Her heart pinged a little, wishful thinking rising up within her own chest. She'd always wanted a sibling. Anyone else to feel a special connection too. Family that she could open up to and share her deepest regrets, hopes, and dreams with. Instead, she'd grown up with a father who'd not stuck around for her first birthday and a mom who'd been too busy finding her latest love on every corner to pay any mind to her only daughter. It had left her determined to only marry once. To find that one *genuine* love, just not a love that would do. *Yeah, and didn't that turn out well.*

Noah bent at the knee, his gaze dropping to meet hers. "Where did you go?"

She shook off her thoughts. Her past was just that, her past. Now was the time for looking forwards and her future: her business.

Walking over to her desk, she did a quick check of her appointment book. There were no fittings sched-uled until tomorrow afternoon. She had planned to work on initial toiles and patterns in the morning for her next collection, but as she was slightly ahead of schedule still, that could be pushed. "Fine. I'll come tomorrow."

"Hallelujah. I'll pick you up?"

The excitement that shone on Noah's face surprised Bekka. "Okay. Sure. Now you need to go so I can get through even more work." She scooted around some boxes filled with trim, lace, and embroidery samples and over to a filing cabinet. A pale blue file sat on top with Valerie's name printed neatly on the label. "Here are the sketches." She turned, not expecting Noah to have followed her. He was right there, in her personal space. His signature scent of spice, cinnamon, and fresh male skin unchanged. Did she really recognize his smell? The memory jolted, leaving an uneasy feeling in her tummy.

He took the folder from her, his brows raised. "You okay?"

"Yep. Super. I'll see you at eight tomorrow morning."

"Eight-thirty. Sure I can't walk your dog or do something to help?" he persisted, not moving an inch from where he stood. She was wedged between his big male frame and the cabinet behind her. As if sensing a mention, Smooch gave a little yip that was muffled from behind the door. The world was conspiring against her.

Noah glanced over to the door that led into her

home quarters. A smug grin settled on his face. "Smooch seems keen?"

"You really want to walk my dog?"

"Sure. Why not? I often walk Mom's at home."

"I didn't know you liked dogs," Bekka commented, sidestepping out from her spot to walk over and open the door. Smooch shot through, but instead of coming to her as he usually would, he headed straight to Noah, jumping up on his hind legs to lean against Noah's shins. His tail wagged in delight.

Noah crouched, rubbing a hand over the left side of the dog's cheek and scratching him under the ear. Just the spot Bekka knew Smooch loved. "Yeah, I do. Grew up with enough of them running about the place. Mom's been a breeder for years. I've toyed with the idea of getting my own for a while now, I'm just hesitant given the job. It's been a lot of travel in the past few years."

"That doesn't sound ideal for a dog. A cat, maybe." She smiled. "Why do you need to travel so much? I thought you were just helping your dad out with a few things before you start your own hotel. Or isn't that the plan now?"

Noah sighed, and she sensed her question hit a nerve. Smooch scooted down, rolling over and snuggling at Noah's hand as it shifted its administrations. Her puppy was putty in Noah's gigantic hands.

"I still want too. That's the secret squirrel part of my visit." He flicked his gaze to hers, his eyes a deep green with a serious over sheen. "I still want my hotel, to build my mark in the industry, but Dad's now talking retirement. With an expectation I'll just step in." He shook his head, a grimace pulling the corner of his lips up. "Clark's stepped into the financial role but doesn't want to run the place. Dad suddenly has this view of how it will all pan out and expects we'll all be happy about it."

Bekka kneeled down, running a hand over Smooch's upturned snout. "You don't want to disappoint him by saying no."

"No. I don't."

"That's tough. I wish I could offer some advice, but honestly, I'm the least qualified with family. That would require having a family that cared enough to take an interest." She smiled to soften her harsh opinion. Even if it was true.

Noah stared at her for a while, and Bekka felt the mood shift.

"I'd love to know more about your upbringing someday, Bekka. But you've really made something of your life. I'm glad you took a chance on your business. You were wasting your design talent studying business just to work in an office somewhere."

Bekka threw Noah an arch look. "You were always so disdainful of my designing at college."

"No. I was in awe of your talents you appeared to be planning to just throw away. You half started a business but shied away from putting everything into it, like you were just using it as a waiting position instead of believing in yourself."

Bekka mulled over Noah's words. They made sense, strangely. She'd never really understood why Noah had seemed to always disapprove of her actions while they were all studying together, but maybe she'd also imagined some of it. That had been Connor's views whenever she'd discussed the problem with him.

Connor believed the sun rose and fell with Noah Fox. He'd been a smitten friend, and Bekka was now mature enough to admit that his behavior towards Noah had annoyed her. Any behavior that turned someone into a simpering mimic of another person infuriated her. It spoke of weakness to her. Which was what her mom had been her entire life. Chasing after one man or the next. Changing her life, her views, even down to the smallest insignificant opinion like not liking peas if only to please her latest beau.

"Thanks." Bekka murmured, deciding she needed to say something to fill the void.

"All right. Smooch, do you have a leash? Let's go explore. Is there a route you normally take him on?"

They both straightened, but Bekka stumbled, warmth flooding up her arms as Noah's arm steadied her. She mentally shook her head, pretending the odd awareness of Noah was just because they hadn't seen each other in years. It was nothing more than that. Nothing.

"Turn left out the front, then I normally go down

two blocks, and loop around. Try to avoid the main restaurant strip as he goes a little mad at the smells." Bekka walked back to the door, unhooking the leash from her home side of the wall. She held it out to Noah to take.

"I don't blame him. I noticed a gorgeous little Italian place from the taxi. Is that still your favorite?" He ducked down to clip the leash into place at Smooch's collar, who had sat dutifully the moment the leash had materialized.

Bekka's brows rose, surprised that he remembered that about her. "Yes. I still have a crazy fascination with Italy and it's cuisine."

"Have you been?"

The word 'yet,' hung in the air. She shrugged, her nose scrunching. "One day. I promised myself I'd put everything into building Something Blue into a premier bridal studio, to cement my position as one of the best. Financial security, solid clientele, etcetera. I'm not prepared to go running off on a vacation until I meet those goals."

He twisted the leash about his fingers, folding the leather end this way and that. "Well, perhaps you'll let me take you out to a delicious Italian dinner at least. It's not Rome, but it looked very authentic."

She took too long to answer. Her immediate answer of yes had stalled on her tongue.

The corner of his mouth quirked, his eyes sparkling with mischief that made him ten times more handsome, which didn't seem fair. "Just have a think about it." He scooped up Smooch and walked back down the corridor and out the front door. The lock clicking back into place on the pale blue door seemed somehow ominous.

Don't be daft, Bekka. Time to just get back to work.

Unable to get Bekka's words out of his mind, Noah fished his phone out of his jeans pocket and hit dial when he came to Connor's number. Smooch set off on a speedy trot, his nose taking him in zig-zag patterns across the sidewalk. After a few rings, the call connected.

"Noah. How are you? Are you stateside, yet?"

"Hey mate. My flight came in last weekend. Do you have a moment?"

"Of course, you sound rather formal? Is something the matter?"

"Why did you never tell me you ran into Bekka about a month after you called off the wedding?"

Connor swallowed audibly down the phone line. "Ah well, it didn't seem that important. Who told you that?"

"Bekka did." Noah returned flatly.

"Bekka? You've seen her?"

"She's designing my sister's dress."

"Oh yeah? Good for her. I heard her business was

doing well. We must take your sister and her fiancé out for a meal when I come to New York. I'm still keen to meet Arnold, I know I mentioned it—"

"Connor." Noah cut the other man off, "you told Bekka it was my idea. You put the blame fair and square in my court. After you wouldn't even tell her, you couldn't marry her yourself. Why?"

"I think that's exaggerating."

"Bekka told me she broke down in public, and you admitted you couldn't go through with the wedding because *I'd* told you not to marry her. Are you saying that's not what happened?"

Silence stretched. Noah could still hear Connor's breathing interspersed with the occasional sniff and huff.

"Fine. That's what I told her. I couldn't handle her tears and that was easier than telling her I just didn't want to get married."

"Throwing your friend under the bus was easier than telling the truth?" Noah pushed.

"Yes. In that instance, it was. Besides, you and Bekka bickered all the time, and you'd said you thought we were making a mistake getting married that young. What's the big deal?"

"The big deal, Connor, is that Bekka hasn't spoken to me in five years—has turned down every olive branch I've given her—because of a lie you told. I nearly lost her friendship because of you."

"Oh. Sorry. I didn't realize you two were actually

friends." Connor's tone had changed, taking on a weird edge.

"I didn't enjoy being the one to deliver your news. Afterward, she stopped taking my calls. I had to fly home to help Dad and after that, she never once spoke to me again. It was awkward."

"Yeah, I can see your point. Anyway. All behind us now, in the past and all that. How long are you in town?"

Noah huffed internally, frustrated that Connor didn't seem to see that what he'd done was wrong. They spoke for a little longer before Noah hung up.

He hated that he'd been the one to turn up on Bekka's doorstep and break her heart. Connor had outright refused to go speak to her, having packed a bag and decided to just skip town instead of facing the fallout. Noah had lost a lot of respect for his friend that day and there was no way he would allow Bekka to go through thinking the wedding was still going ahead when he knew Connor would not attend, so he'd done what he thought was best.

Except it had put him in the most impossible position of breaking Bekka's heart. A heart that wasn't even his, though he'd wanted it to be.

Sucking in a deep breath, he pushed thoughts of Connor aside. It was years ago now. Bekka herself had said that Connor wasn't right for her, a fact she said she now realized. Which meant he had a clean slate to work from to show her they'd always been an excellent match. If only she'd allow herself to see that.

Smooch turned left, appearing to know his dog walk route by heart. Noah whistled a tune, deciding to just enjoy his time out and about with a cute dog. The air was crisp and clear, though marred with the unmistakable smell of New York. He sent Valerie a quick text, letting her know he was on task. He thought about calling his father and then changed his mind. He'd done his fill of hard conversations for the day, plus he'd told Valerie he'd come to help her with her wedding prep and to spend time with her on his trip. He'd left out the argument he'd had with his father prior to leaving, one that centered on the business.

He understood that his reluctance to take over the helm of Fox Holdings surprised his father. Their premium and exclusive boutique hotels were in a few choice locations around Australia, but there'd always been talk of expansion. Well, Noah had always spoken of expansion. His father didn't understand why on earth he'd want to expand anywhere other than Australia. Two of the hotels were in Sydney, which is where his parents lived and where he'd spent part of the past five years helping. He'd come to the university in America because he wanted to see more of the world, and since his mother was American, it had seemed a great place to start. He hadn't expected to lose his heart on the first day of the semester. Not to a smiley, fresh-faced girl-next-door type who was already spoken for.

He could still recall those first five minutes of chat with Bekka Arden, his heart beating an uneven tattoo in his chest, his words tripping over themselves. She'd been sitting alone on a wooden bench seat, a sketch-book laid across her lap as her pencil ran furiously across the page. He'd stood off to the side, intrigued by how engrossed in her task she was when people streamed all around her. He'd always loved people watching, and she'd enraptured him. He'd approached and had repeated an introduction no less than three times before he'd been able to draw her attention from her work. By then he'd been able to make out her design sketches. Ungainly slim and tall figures sheathed in elegant gowns. Her attention to detail had jumped off the page, as had her enthusiasm that shone in those brown eyes when they'd finally glanced up at him.

He'd sat, soaking in her sunshine smiles and soft words, only to fall flat when Connor had appeared, his arm sweeping Bekka in close as he pressed a kiss to her nose.

Noah ignored the crush at first, hiding behind sardonic glances and often harsh criticism. He couldn't understand how someone with her talent could want to choose business with a view to major in accounting. His frustration had grown when she'd become engaged to Connor just months before their graduation. She'd made a few dresses for friends, one of which had even ended up in Vogue magazine. The cards were all there for her to start her business with a bang, and yet all she'd done was dabble. When he'd confronted her about her ideas, she'd said that starting a business of any magnitude was a silly goal, since she planned to marry Connor in the Fall and start a family straight away.

His gut had churned at her wide-eyed innocence and ignorance. Connor wanted to travel, to go see the world, and yet he'd proposed to his girlfriend who was already planning their family complete with a white picket fence and dog.

Perhaps his words to Connor about being truthful and the importance of communication had pushed his friend to see that proposing had been the wrong thing to do? Noah felt sick at the thought he'd indirectly caused Bekka such pain, and more than anything he hated that her fledgling business had ended because of it.

Now she was back on top and seemed to give the business her all. He only hoped that she'd give him the same second chance.

CHAPTER 5

The table was filled with cake. Bekka started mentally counting the plates, giving up after she reached fourteen. Were they really going to taste *all* of these?

Noah's grin spread so wide across his face she worried it would snap in two.

"Is this your idea of heaven?" Bekka joked.

"It's close. Very, very close."

Noah stepped forward, bending over the table and taking an elaborate sniff. The cakes were arranged graded by color and she assumed flavor combinations. This would be an experience to remember.

"Bonjour!" A flamboyant red-headed man swooped down the spiral staircase that was center stage within the warehouse space. The location had initially raised Bekka's interest, not picking this to be where a New York premiere cake designer would be based, but the moment she'd stepped inside she understood. The high ceilings and large uncluttered interior were airy and light. There was plenty of room to mosey around and relax. This room had a smattering of furniture, the big wooden table with the cakes, and a comfortable white lounge set off to the side. The cold, urban styling contrasted with the intricately beautiful and inspired cakes on display. The staircase heralded a wrought-iron railing that looked delicate and masculine all at once—the detail immediately giving Bekka new ideas for her range.

"Noah Fox." Noah stretched a hand out which was swiped aside as the man embraced him in a giant hug before moving on and engulfing Bekka in a similar welcome.

"I hug. Pierre Humbert at your service." He added with a flourish of his hand. "You are Bekka Arden. I hear *ahmazing* things. I'm surprised it's taken this long for our paths to cross."

Heat crept up her neck and she cupped her jaw with her hands, hoping to still any further spread. "Thank you. I don't think I need to say your cakes are out of this world and inspired. I'm so excited to be tasting today."

"You are neither the bride nor the groom, no?" His shrewd gaze flicked between the two.

"My sister is the bride, Valerie Fox." Noah piped up. His gaze kept sneaking back to the cakes on the table as though he just wanted to dive in.

"Oh yes. The wedding of the year, to Arnold Hemming. Lucky lady, Arnold is a divine looking man."

Noah coughed, but Bekka had the distinct feeling he was covering a slight choke. "I'm yet to meet him."

Pierre shrugged, as though that fact was inconsequential. "Well. Shall we start? I normally have my assistant do tastings, but since you're such valued clients and as a favor to Emilia—you have me all to your lovely selves." He walked around the table to stand on the opposite side, then began pointing at plates and rattling off flavors. Hazelnut chocolate mud, triple choc seventy percent dark mud, classic dark chocolate mud, black forest cake, fine crumb milk, and white swirl cake... the list was endless, and he was still only pointing at the brown cake selection. Bekka wondered if it would be rude to ask for a chair. If she would taste this many cakes, she wanted to sit.

"Should we sit here or we can take a few samples over to the couches? I usually encourage a long tasting. No need to rush through. Emilia said Valerie requested the full tasting. Mentioned someone had a sweet tooth?"

Noah meekly raised a hand, his grin spreading at the look of satisfaction that crossed Pierre's face. "Let's take the couches, I might need to be seated for this experience."

Bekka laughed and silently apologized to her body. She'd be running for days to work off the calories that were awaiting her. The smell alone told her every bite would be worth it.

Pierre sliced off sizeable chunks of cake, placing them on pristine white fine bone china plates that were spaced out across a gilt-edged trolley. He wielded the cake server tools as though they were part of him, and Bekka found herself quite enraptured by the process. He escorted them to the lounges, which enveloped Bekka like a cloud the moment she sat.

Her first bite of the chocolate mud torte cake left her moaning. "Oh my! This is heaven. Choose this one." Bekka delivered, diving back in for a second mouthful. Even after she'd promised herself she'd only have one of each.

Noah stabbed a forkful into his mouth and chewed, a thoughtful expression crossing his face. "That's definitely good. But I'm reserving judgment for now."

Bekka's eyes widened. *How could anything possibly taste better?*

"Smart man, this one," Pierre said with satisfaction.

The rest of the tasting passed in a blur of deliciousness that threatened to pull Bekka into a sugar coma. After the seventh cake that tasted just as sensational as the one before, she gave up any pretense of being able to choose and just enjoyed herself. Noah, on the other hand, was taking this all too seriously. He'd cracked out a notebook to jot down notes after the fourth cake, glaring off her initial giggle. The man really took his cake seriously.

Noah held the piece of cheesecake at the back of his tongue, rolling it around to savor every last drop of cheesy deliciousness. Cheesecake wasn't an option for the entire cake, but Noah had noted it down as a groom's cake option, perhaps as part of a cheeseboard tower or some such. Valerie had given him free rein in this department, and he intended to take full advantage of that.

Even if it was earning him amused glances from Bekka.

He looked over at her now, a spoon dangling from her peachy pink glossy lips as she sucked the last bite of cake off. Her wavy chocolate hair was pulled into a loose ponytail, the ends curling temptingly at the center of her back. She was dressed casually in slim-fit jeans and a white shirt, her feet in flat shoes covered in flowers. This whole outing was a little torturous, seeing her take bite after bite of cake. He admitted to feeling a touch of envy towards her spoon.

"Cheesecake isn't usually a popular choice for a tall cake, but I couldn't resist adding this to the tasting. Thoughts?" Pierre asked, his eyes flicking between the two.

Bekka moaned an affirmative noise around her spoon, which still hadn't left her mouth.

Noah focused on the cakes before them. "Delicious. I'd like to incorporate it, I'm thinking groom's cake?"

"Excellent choice. Shall I give you two some time to think over the choice for the main cake?"

"Please," he nodded.

Bekka smiled as Pierre moved away. The other man had a way about him.

"How do you even choose?" Her brows knitted together as she assessed the cakes.

"Easy. Seven tiers, each of the different mud cake varieties. Layers joined with the dark chocolate ganache and the outside covered with the whipped and whitened vanilla-bean buttercream. White chocolate floral work and gold painted tuile biscuit leaves cascading down one side and across the top."

Her mouth dropped open as he spoke, her eyes widening with each word. They were the exact color of the melted chocolate sauce he'd spooned onto the side of this plate. But ever more delicious.

"Are you sure you're in the right industry?" Her tinkling laugh followed her words.

"I am. But like I said, cake's my thing."

"Evidently. Is your mom sad she's not here to help?"

The change in subject threw him a little, as did the slight veil that seemed to slip over Bekka's face.

"Yes. But she also knows that Valerie's a bit of a force with getting what she wants. She's probably also happy to be out of the firing line. They'll arrive at the end of the month, so still plenty of time to enjoy the festivities before the main event."

"Festivities?" Bekka queried.

"This isn't just a wedding, it's a whole circus." He smiled. "Why do you ask about my mom?"

He remembered his mom had taken a real shine to Bekka the only time she'd met her.

"Just popped into my head. I always wonder how parents feel when their babes take this step. It's a big one."

"It is."

"I'm surprised some lady hasn't locked you down, actually."

He swallowed. He hadn't been a saint in the dating department, but no woman had ever sent his heart flipping like Bekka did. A fact he'd never been game enough to utter to anyone, but now he was actually here... well... *now or never, right?*

"I've been waiting for the right woman." His eyes locked with hers, his not wavering even when a slight frown slid across her features.

"I'm sure she's out there." The corners of her mouth lifted in a smile, but it was strained. Not the normal carefree one that had graced her features for most of the morning.

"How about you?"

"I'm on a dating hiatus. Besides, between dragging my business back into the black, Smooch, and my NBC friends, I don't have a minute to spare."

He frowned. "NBC friends?"

Her eyes scrunched tight along with her nose. "Friends. Ignore the NBC part."

"Oh no. That cannot be ignored. I'm assuming it stands for something?"

"It may. But I'm not telling you what."

"Can I guess?"

"You can try." Her eye roll spoke volumes, which only made him more determined.

"Hmm. NBC… Naughty bra club?"

"What! No, of course not!" Her voice pitched in shock.

"No bra—"

"Don't finish that thought."

"No boy's club?"

She sighed. "You're not giving up on this, are you?"

"No. But how about this: you tell me, and I promise not to breathe a word to another soul?"

"Fine." She beckoned for him to lean in so she could whisper in his ear. "No Brides Club."

Noah spluttered. "The No Brides Club? Did I hear you correctly?"

Her hands flew to her cheeks, trying to cover the red tinge that was blossoming there. "Uh huh."

"Seriously?" he exclaimed. "But weddings and brides are your career. You've always wanted the big white wedding and eternal love deal. You don't want that anymore?"

Unease had him clenching his fists. A sick feeling that had nothing to do with eating too much cake settled in his gut.

"I don't. After Connor, well, it made me realize that it's not for me."

"You're joking. Please tell me you're joking. You're walking away from love because of what he did to you?"

"You still don't get it, do you?" She rose then, fury vibrating about her, and she stalked away to the window, her arms crossed as though holding herself together. "Connor walking away from me didn't just break my career, it broke my dreams."

He expected her words to be clipped and full of anger, but it was worse than that. They were quiet, her tone broken. He knew then that he had a long road ahead of him.

That day still haunted him, having to tell her that Connor was calling off the wedding and yet, she hadn't shed one tear. At least, not in his presence. She'd been shaken, and a little pale, but he thought she'd taken the news remarkably well. It was becoming increasingly clear that that was not the case at all. She just hadn't confided in him. She'd fallen apart, and he'd been none the wiser. He hated himself for leaving her like that.

He'd been hurting in his own way. He'd spent every year of college watching and waiting to see if cracks would appear in Bekka's feelings for Connor, but they hadn't. She'd been so steadfast and committed, he'd convinced himself that his feelings didn't matter. He would see her married to another, and he made his peace with that.

But now?

He shook his head. "Don't do this, Bekka. Don't let him take your dreams. Almost from the moment I met you, I knew two things. One: you were an extremely talented designer and were wasting your time chasing a career in accounting. Two: you wanted the fairy tale. Love was the one belief that never shook you, even coming from a broken family. Now you're telling me you're just going to walk away from that?"

She spun to him, her hip cocked, and a brow raised. "Well, it's easy for you, isn't it, Noah? A loving upbringing, you can take a broken heart now and then. I can't, okay? My mom was right, I was barking up the wrong tree. Connor was always going to choose better things than me." She glanced at her watch. "I need to get going. Do you still need me here?"

Yes! Always! But he spoke neither. "I'll call you a cab."

Bekka leaned her head back against the pleather headrest, berating herself. *Silly, silly, silly.* Noah's honesty—though brutal—still shook her like no one else. How did he still do that? How did he see inside her?

Collecting her phone from her bag, she pulled up her mother's number and just stared at the screen. What number husband was she up to now? Seven? Eight? Each her 'true and forever love'. *'I've found him this time, Bekka. For good. I just feel it in my heart.'*

How often had her mother said those words? A dreamy, faraway look in her eyes, the world at her fingertips. Every time a piece of Bekka's heart had hardened, vowing to never just throw herself into the first depths of attraction. Only genuine love would turn her head and her heart.

And look how that had turned out.

She'd been so sure about Connor. So trusting that they had been one hundred percent solid. His proposal had been beyond romantic, and she'd allowed herself to be swept away in the moment.

The only person who hadn't been over the moon happy for them was Noah.

Why was it she could only vaguely remember her own reaction to Connor's proposal, the memories foggy and smudged around the edges, yet Noah's slight frown still stuck clear in her head?

Perhaps she needed to tell Noah about her upbringing, like he'd expressed an interest in hearing. He knew that her father hadn't stuck around, but she'd told no one about the revolving door of her mother's heart. Which was the real reason that after being burned by Connor, she wouldn't risk falling in love again. Focusing on her business was far less risky.

It took Noah another hour before he could tie up all the details with Pierre. The cake order was completed,

Valerie had been duly informed of his choices and had squealed in delight when he'd spoken to her. His hand still clutched his phone, hanging limp beside him as he walked along the street. He should call a cab, he was miles from where he was staying at Valerie's apartment, but being outside and just listlessly walking in any direction was helping him sort his jumble of thoughts.

He hadn't factored in that Bekka would be so broken—still—from Connor's idiocy. He could punch his friend in the face for the way he'd treated Bekka and had threatened too. They still spoke, but there was a gap in their friendship that Noah felt more than ever. One that had nothing to do with distance. Noah had returned to Australia shortly after the complete debacle and had thrown himself into working for his father, hoping to block out his own part in the disaster. Underlying it all were still his feelings for Bekka that just refused to lie down and drift away.

He'd dated other women, tried hard to forget her, but everyone he compared to her. And no one held up.

John, his father, had called during the cake tasting and he knew he should return the call. Soon too before it would be too late given the time difference.

"Noah."

One clipped response, then a weighted pause. Noah let out a soft sigh. "Dad. Sorry I was helping Valerie."

"Isn't she in San Francisco with Arnold?"

"Yes. That's why I'm helping her. Cake tasting."

His father grunted. "You do have a sweet tooth. That's nice of you to help her."

Noah grimaced, feeling the slight disapproval through the phone. He chose not to bring up their argument, he'd made his choice to come out here and help Valerie and was sticking to it. He missed their usual closeness though, and ease of conversation. It seemed his father was also sick of the elephant in the room.

"We need to talk about the business, son. I know you said your piece before you left, but I need an answer."

Fingers reached out and clutched at his heart, squeezing the air out.

"I'm still thinking it over. I love the business, you know I do, but I never envisaged myself as staying in Sydney to take over the helm there this early. I want to give myself time to start my own branch here in New York. I have three possible sites—"

"So you're saying no."

"Dad," he sighed, "I'm not saying no. I'm saying I still need to think it over. What is the sudden rush to lock this in place? I didn't think you wanted to retire yet?"

There was a long pause, and Noah wasn't sure that his father wouldn't just hang up. "Your mom's fall… I guess it's just put some things into perspective."

The words held lead so heavy they weighed Noah down from the other side of the world. "Dad, why didn't you say that's what has you so worried? It was just a tumble. Mom's already hobbling around."

"That's how it started with your grandfather, son. First a fall, which he brushed off. A month later he had a heart attack and suddenly I had a business thrust onto my shoulders. I don't want that for you, I don't want you swamped with responsibility you aren't ready or prepared for."

Noah turned left down a side street and slumped onto the first brick wall that came into sight. "Dad… grandfather was well into his seventies. I know his passing took you by surprise. It shook all of us—even at eight I could see the ramifications—but you're not your father. I know the business inside and out. I've spent the past five years within each of the depart- ments, staying within each of the hotels. I think the bigger question here is, are you ready? You need not give up the top job to go take a proper holiday with mom. Take a month, go on a cruise, go island hopping. Heck, take the Winnebago you bought last year and travel to Western Australia. Wi-fi is a miraculous thing, plus Clark is there."

"Clark looks after finance, he's terrible with people. You know that."

Noah rolled his eyes. His younger brother could be best described as an introvert, but that didn't mean he couldn't manage the company for a few months if their parents took a break. "How about this? You promise to spend the next month re-thinking early retirement and

I promise to spend the next month deciding on my exact future plans?"

Again with the gigantic sigh. "Okay. I'll expect links to these supposed amazing locations within the hour."

He heard his father's smile before the call ended.

It wasn't that he didn't want to take over the business; it was just that right now he couldn't let go of the possibility of Bekka, and she was firmly planted in New York. Before he gave up on that dream he had to at least give it a go, and there was no time like the present to show her that love was well and truly still alive.

If only she'd open her eyes and see him standing right before her.

CHAPTER 6

It was another week before Bekka ran into Noah again. She'd spent that time berating herself on her over-reaction. Noah was only trying to help. Just because she was a little touchy on the subject of love didn't mean she needed to brush off an old friendship.

Oddly, she realized she missed him.

Yesterday she'd received a cake delivery. It was petite, and almost too good to eat. A delicious white chocolate mud mound topped with a vibrant pink chocolate flower. The accompanying note on thick parchment held one word—sorry—signed with N.

She hadn't allowed herself to acknowledge missing any of her college friends since her life, as she'd known it back then, had imploded. But the cake tasting had brought back some of those feelings. It had been equally delicious and full of relaxed banter. She had a multitude of girlfriends from joining the No Brides Club, but Noah knew her from before. Her life was full, and she considered herself happy, and yet there was still a tinge of bitterness that shadowed all her thoughts. She'd not had that during college.

Noah hadn't been her best friend, most of the time they'd taken opposing sides on any topic of conversation, but she could always count on him and he's always been honest. He'd been part of their small group of friends. Connor, herself, Noah, and two others from business school. She'd broken ties with all of them after Connor's betrayal. They'd been more his friends than hers, anyway.

Hadn't she always felt just that little distanced within the group? Noah had been the only one she'd kept tabs on after her non-wedding and business implosion, even after running into Connor and having him lay the blame at Noah's feet—he was the only one she'd wanted to know about. She refused to let herself follow any information that would lead to Connor.

Smooch yipped at her feet, signaling she'd been standing at the front door holding his leash more than long enough.

"Okay, okay. We'll go walk."

The air whooshed past her as she stepped out, collecting up the sides of her skirt and sending it flying in a Marilyn Monroe air grate style. Her screech was scarily similar to Smooch's.

"Now there's a sight."

Bekka gulped. "Noah! Hi." She glanced up, taking in his calf-length black coat with the collar pulled up that half hid a pristine black suit. The wind flicked his sandy blond hair across his forehead and into his eyes before he flicked it away with one finger.

"Hi yourself. You'll cause a traffic jam if you head out in that skirt." He remarked.

Her cheeks grew hot. "Can you take Smooch for a minute, I need to go change." Before giving him time to answer, she shoved the dog leash into his hands and dashed back inside. Three minutes later, clad in more appropriate jeans, she reemerged to find Noah crouched over Smooch giving him belly rubs.

"My dog really loves you."

He stood, a seriously cute smirk in place. "I have a way."

She rolled her eyes. "I was just taking him for his walk. Did you want to join us? Or did you have something urgent you needed for Valerie?"

He held his arm out, ushering her down the path, and they started walking down the street. "I'd love to accompany you two beautiful ladies on your walk."

"Smooch is a boy, you know that right? You're in a good mood."

Noah chuckled, then shrugged. "I found the perfect location." He all but burst with excitement, like a little boy the night before Christmas.

Her brows knitted together. "Perfect location for what?"

His hand stilled her movements, turning her to face him. "My expansion of the Luxury Fox Boutique hotels. I found a place on Long Island. Seventeen bedroom mansion, right on the water, with its own personal pontoon."

Bekka whistled. "Wow. I bet that will cost a pretty penny."

"Possibly but the potential is astronomical. We've been asked so often about locations abroad. New York is one of the top cities our regular clients visit—part business and because the wives love it—but this would be the ultimate fit for that. It's not right in the city, but we could have a driver on site."

She noticed he let his words fade, his focus drifting off to stare over her shoulder. Turning a little, she couldn't see anything particularly fascinating and realized he was lost in his own thoughts and imagination.

"You're picturing it, aren't you? Every room to your specifications, the gardens, right down to the uniform?" she smiled.

His focus flew back to her. "How did you know?"

"I do exactly the same when an idea comes to me. Did you see it this morning?"

Smooch tugged at the leash, pulling them back into a leisurely walk. "Not yet. It's not yet on the market. I've been working with a real estate agent who is keeping an eye out for me. Do you remember Ben from college?"

"Only vaguely."

"His girlfriend is in real estate, works for some big firm in the city but she found this beauty and let me know. For the right buyer, they said they are happy to take an offer before putting it on the market. It's a reluctant sale, financial troubles, but they want to see it go to the right person. I'm meeting them Saturday. I wondered if you'd care to join me?"

"Oh!" she blinked rapidly. Her initial response of yes threatened to spill from the tip of her tongue, but she swallowed it back. "I'm really swamped." A truth, but she could work tonight, she supposed.

"Please? I really value your opinion."

She looked at him, his face a mask. "Why?"

"Because you won't be afraid to rein me in if I'm being an idiot."

She weighed up his words. "I'm not the same person I was back then, Noah. I've changed."

"Changed so much that you won't help me make a life-changing decision? Come on Bekka, you are the one person I can rely on to always be one hundred percent honest with me. Remember when we did that group assignment on business relations? The others in our group deferred to me since we chose my father's business. Only you spoke up and told me when you thought something was wrong. Reluctantly the others did too, though they waited until later to tell me. After you'd proven your point." The corner of his mouth pulled up.

"Well, you *were* wrong."

"Please, Bekka. I really want us to be good friends again and good friends hang out."

Bekka bit her tongue. Did she want to spend more time with Noah?

"College was years ago, Noah. This is a real estate purchase and major decision for your family's business. I think it's something you should do with family."

Bekka had expected Noah to agree, to move on from his suggestion, but she was wrong. The corners of his mouth dropped, and his steps slowed a little.

"My father knows what I want to do, but he's not totally on board. I have told no one else that I've found the perfect location. Please, Bekka, this would mean a lot to me if you'd come."

His words reached a place deep inside her. How often had she wished she'd had someone to make decisions with, the enor*mous* ones to do with her business in the past few years? After Connor, she'd walked away from all of her friendships from college and school. It was only recently that she'd met the No Brides Club women, who were proving to be saviors in her life, but did that mean she should turn down Noah's request? She couldn't claim she wasn't at all interested, Noah's family business had always intrigued her. How everything was run by family, close and extended. What she wouldn't give to have grown up in such a loving and supportive environment.

"Okay."

"Really?" Noah half spun, a giant smile crossing his face.

"Yes, really." She rolled her eyes, secretly delighted by the enthusiasm shown by him.

Smooch yipped, evidently sensing the excitement in his walkers and their distraction from the task at hand.

"I'll pick you both up Saturday."

"Both?" she frowned.

"You and Smooch. We like to offer our clients a pet-friendly option."

"Seriously? You want me to bring my dog?"

"Absolutely. And now I'd love to hear how you came to name him. You said you'd tell me."

"Are you sure you don't have somewhere else you have to be? Work you need to be doing?" she countered.

"Trying to get rid of me?"

No. Though she was beginning to realize that Noah being back was becoming highly distracting and was putting a dent in her work hours.

"Why did you name your dog Smooch? You promised." Noah raised a brow, pinning Bekka in place.

"That's not exactly what I promised. But okay. I didn't name him, he came with that name and to be honest, I couldn't bring myself to change it."

"Was the dog a gift?"

"Of sorts. He's from a restaurant in Soho. I went there a few times when I was scouting locations for opening my new store, after... well anyway, I went in for lunch and sat outside in the courtyard and there he was. He was only a tiny puppy then. The owner had only just gotten him from the breeder and had him at the restaurant because they were slammed. He came and laid over my shoe and went to sleep. Stayed there the whole time. Because I was looking in the area, I started chatting with the owner who gave me some tips about the location. Then I left."

Noah nodded, waiting to hear more if his appearance was anything to go by.

"So then you dognapped him?"

"Funny. Of course, I didn't. I went back about a week later, I was tossing up between this location and the one in Soho. Soho was gorgeous, much bigger than this, but rent was also a lot more and didn't have the living area attachment like this one. I went in just to grab a coffee and the owner recognized me, asked me to wait a minute. I thought he was a bit crazy but anyway, he went out back then came back through with the puppy who bounded out of his arms and came straight to me. He sat at my feet and whimpered until I picked him up and then he just curled up, doing his little doggy sigh and went straight to sleep. The owner told me on the spot he was mine."

"Seriously?"

"Yep. I tried to protest and was told it was pointless. That Smooch had apparently become depressed and howled the moment I'd left. It had taken the owner a while to work it out, but seeing the puppy reaction when I'd returned had cemented the idea. I offered to pay for him, but again was turned down. So after all of that, I couldn't say no to keeping him, or change his name."

Smooch, as though understanding they were discussing him, turned and put his front paws up onto Bekka's legs. Letting out a soft laugh, she scooped his hind legs up so he could cuddle in her arms, his little nose nuzzling against her chest in adoration.

"He seems smitten."

Bekka looked down at the little brown-eyed ball of fur. "It's mutual. He's the only male I need around right now."

Giving Smooch one last snuggle, she popped him back down before they continued walking.

"Only male you need, hey?" Noah remarked after they'd walked in silence for a bit.

"Yes." She confirmed with a solid head nod for emphasis.

"That's decisive. Is this part of your club rules?"

Bekka sighed. "No. Not exactly. The club started with a group of women who wanted to focus on their careers, putting career goals before love. It doesn't mean we don't date. I guess after Connor, I'm just not sure I'm cut out for the big love anymore. I've lost my faith in it. I have been on dates occasionally since him, but it's always felt forced and I decided that my focus needed to be on me and only me. My career, my business... its everything to me now."

Smooch chose that moment to sprint off. The leash was yanked from her fingers as the little ball of caramel and cream fur flew off toward a tree ahead, barking and yipping at an unknown foe. It took a moment for Bekka to spot the squirrel darting around at the base, which took off like a rocket, Smooch not far behind.

"Oh, no! Smooch!" She broke into a jog, Noah quickly overtaking her. Running was not her forte, and she groaned as both squirrel and dog rounded the corner up ahead.

She followed around two more corners, only just keeping Noah, dog, and squirrel in sight.

Breathing ragged, she closed the distance to another corner, well behind Noah who appeared to have become a sprinter since she'd last known him. Who knew a man running in a suit would be an attractive sight?

Finally reaching the corner, she slowed to a walk as she spotted Noah up ahead, holding a wriggling but contained Smooch. He was cuddling the dog, appearing to murmur as he stroked Smooch's head. A slim woman in skin-tight workout clothes stood with him. Bekka held her tummy, a cramp curling into existence.

Noah waved, an impish smile on his face.

Her stride lagging, she attempted to drag in some deeper breathes and get her body under control. Who on earth was workout Barbie?

"Such a gorgeous doggy." The blonde cooed as Bekka came into hearing range.

"Not mine, unfortunately. He belongs to this lovely lady." Noah held a hand towards Bekka.

Lovely lady? Did he mean her? Looking like a bedraggled, unfit, crazy person?

"Oh!" Blondie said, giving Bekka the once over. "What a lucky woman."

Bekka couldn't be sure if the other lady was referring to her or Smooch.

"Well, if things don't work out…" Blondie pulled a card from between her skin-tight exercise bra, and Bekka balked as she shamelessly handed it to Noah.

The words 'we aren't together' died on her lips. Instead, she sent the other woman an insincere smile as she collected Smooch from Noah's arms.

"Thanks," she murmured after Blondie had sauntered off.

"You're welcome." Noah was giving her an odd enquiring look.

"What?" she scoffed.

"Nothing." He held his hands up, "If I didn't know better, I'd say there was a hint of jealousy in that smile just now."

"Jealous? Of Malibu Barbie? No thanks."

Noah laughed, a deep sound that came from his belly. His face transformed, and it momentarily stunned Bekka. He'd always been highly attractive, but she'd never really paid attention to it, given she had been happy with Connor. But now… now she was all too aware of just how handsome he was.

Get a grip, Bekka.

∽

Noah fist pumped the air. Bekka had been jealous earlier today. He could see it in the way her chocolate brown eyes had deepened, and gone a little wide, drifting across his face as though dazed. Back in college, all she'd seen was Connor. She had been head over heels for the guy and while Noah liked Connor—they had become great mates—he'd always sensed that Bekka was more invested than Connor was in their relationship.

It had bugged him to no end, how she'd always been so ready to drop whatever she was doing to go help Connor or do what Connor wanted. That wasn't what a relationship should be. It was two people being equals, both bringing love to the table.

Noah had always suspected that Connor had loved Bekka's undivided attention more than he'd loved her.

Their breakup had strained the close friendship that he and Connor had built, particularly when Noah had returned to Sydney shortly after to help his father with the family business.

They'd kept in touch via email and the odd phone call, but not once had Connor mentioned he'd put the blame onto Noah, saying that he'd told Connor to break things off. That jabbed at his ribs and had been needling him ever since Bekka had blurted that out. Speaking to Connor hadn't lessened the frustration.

A ringing sounded from his pocket and he fished it out, connecting the call when he saw Valerie's number.

"Hello, dear sister of mine."

"You're in a good mood," Valerie replied, sounding a little strained.

"I am. I'm enjoying a slower pace, getting to hang out with a beautiful lady, and today I'm off to look at some real estate. What's not to love?"

"Wait, what beautiful lady?"

"Bekka. We've been hanging out a little."

"I thought you said you two were only ever friends."

"We were, but that was then. This is now."

"Is she… you know… the one you've always pined about?"

He jolted at Valerie's words before he gave in. "Yes. She's that one."

"I knew it! There was totally a vibe happening between you two at that first meeting. Tell me everything!"

"Valerie… remember how you called me?"

"Oh! Fine. Spoilsport. I'll get it out of you another time. I have another favor to ask."

"Hit me with it."

"Well, it's not much, really. But I need you to find me a carriage."

Noah choked. "Tell me you're joking."

"No. Well, I don't need you to *find* me one, exactly. More just go test a couple. Emilia has set up the appointments, you just need to arrive for the rides."

"Valerie, may I point out that this is *your* wedding. Don't you want to be around for at least some decisions?"

"I do. And I'm constantly speaking to Emilia and getting updates. I adore the images you sent from Pierre. Bekka and I finalized my dress design and she'll have a first fit ready by mid next week when I get back to New York. The dresses I ordered from Gamballista have arrived for my bridesmaids, and they have all picked them up. It's all on track. But I really want to know what it feels like riding in the carriage, if it's too windy, or cold. Do I need to organize a coat to suit my dress, etc. But I'm not there, so I figured why not you? It's only a brief ride through Central Park."

There were so many responses to his sister's words that he didn't even know where to start, but he tried. "First, a carriage ride... presumably, you mean one pulled by horses? Or at least one horse?"

"There are two, though Emilia said she could find one with four if I wanted bigger."

Heaven help him. "Two sounds plenty."

"Do you think? I want to make an entrance."

"Oh, I'm sure you'll be doing just that."

"Don't be sarcastic, Noah. It doesn't suit you."

He was going to question her more, but then gave up. What was one more minor task? Besides... he'd talked Bekka into the cake tasting with him, and his real estate viewing tomorrow. Maybe she wouldn't mind a brief ride around Central Park.

"When is it?"

"Sunday. Brother, you are the best."

He could only hope Bekka would see him that way too.

CHAPTER 7

*N*oah brought the car to a smooth stop behind an oversized and expensive black SUV, which was parked out the front entrance of the Long Island mansion.

Bekka let out a low whistle. "It's big." Smooch yipped from the backseat as though agreeing.

"Which makes it perfect for turning into a boutique hotel. The groundwork is all there."

"Does that make it easier on the purse strings or harder? I can only imagine this will set you back a lot." Her eyes found his, tension filling hers.

"I've done the numbers, and I'll check them with Clark before I make an offer, but it's looking good. The quick turn-around would mean we can start taking bookings almost instantly, which helps. Usually, the output is high with no return for months. This way I can afford to go higher in the first place."

"That… oddly makes sense."

"Come on. You need to see this view."

Bekka shook her head in wonderment. "I thought you hadn't seen this in person yet."

"I haven't, but I've spent a lot of time on Google maps."

He hopped out and jogged around the front of the rental car to open her door.

"Thanks," Bekka said, a blush stealing over her features. It gave him a warm gooey feeling to have created that glow. He waited for Smooch to jump out also, collecting up the little cavalier and tucking him into his arm.

He knew his excitement levels rivaled that of a young boy the night before Christmas, but he just had a good feeling about this place. So far it was ticking every single box he'd hoped for and being able to see it the first time with Bekka somehow made it even more special.

Collecting her hand, he tangled his fingers with hers and swung their arms in a friendly manner, all the while hoping she wouldn't pull her hand away. The front entrance was grand, the circular driveway perfect for dropping off guests and then valet parking. He knew there to be an enormous expanse of land off to the side, which he could convert into private parking for guests during their stay.

The front door opened inwards by the real estate

agent. Noah put Smooch down, his leash already in place, which Bekka took from him. The real estate agent held out a hand, which Noah gripped, giving it a light shake but not breaking his connection with Bekka.

"Shall I show you around?"

"Actually, do you mind if we just wander?" Noah remarked.

"No problem. I'll be in the kitchen area when you're done or if you have questions."

Noah tugged at Bekka's hand, taking her straight through the large open entrance hall and through to an expansive kitchen, living, and outdoor area. The downstairs rooms were all large and perfectly aligned to setting up as rooms for guests to relax in. All the bedrooms were up on the second and third levels. No elevator, but they'd have a full-time porter to carry bags and they could look at installing an elevator for patrons to use. Smooch sniffed about, trying to pull them in several directions but Bekka held firm.

Walking outside, the air tasted of salt, the giant expanse of water right before them.

"Wow." Bekka's word hung on the tip of her tongue. "This is… something else."

"Gorgeous, right? There's a pool and tennis courts over there," he pointed to an extensive building set off to one side. "The pontoon is private, which means guests could dock their boat there or we could look at yacht trips. I'd set up some outdoor dining here and close off the kitchen so it's not part of the principle thoroughfare."

"It's idyllic."

Smooch yanked on his leash, trying to leap forward and towards the water.

"The rooms are all quite spacious. I'd look at knocking some walls down to bring the room number down. The guests want privacy, and luxury when they choose a Fox boutique experience, they don't want to be tripping over people in the corridors. There are already seven bathrooms, but that would need to be increased to suit the final room count."

"You're visualizing it again, aren't you?" Bekka turned to him, her hand squeezing his.

"Sure am. The building is just amazing. Early nineteen hundreds architecture, but it's as solid as gold. It needs re-painting, and I'd go with navy, cream, and gold highlights. Try to keep the look elegant and sophisticated, but with a homey edge. A similar vibe to our hotel at Sorrento."

"Where's that?"

Noah was so wrapped up in his vision he took a moment to switch back. Bekka was standing with her head cocked to the side, her question reflected in her gaze. He could easily imagine her walking along the pristine beaches around Sorrento, her hair free and floating about her face.

"On the coast of Victoria, right on the water. Also, a stunning location, though that hotel is larger. I want this to be full of grandeur and really accommodate every one of our guest's whims. It's the perfect expansion point for The Luxury Fox."

Bekka squinted a little, which turned to a frown. "But your father doesn't think so?"

Noah let out a small sigh. No, his father wasn't on board yet. A fact which niggled at Noah's conscious constantly. He'd first mentioned the idea just after he'd returned to Australia from the States, and his father had met his ideas with enthusiasm. It hadn't been the right time then from Noah's perspective. He'd wanted to learn all the ins and outs of the company first. Now, it felt right to him. He didn't understand why all of a sudden his father was stalling on the idea. They had the name, the branding, the society connections… his father's choice was baffling. It was as though he was now fighting for Noah to take over the reins for the company and just stand still. That was not want Noah wanted—he wanted to push this company worldwide.

He squared his shoulders. "He will. Once I've completed all the plans, I'll present them to him. It will need to be done soon, and probably over the phone, unless I can convince the seller to hold off on putting it officially on the market."

"I'd have thought your dad would jump at whatever suggestions you make."

Makes two of us. Unsure how to explain his father's odd behavior, Noah shrugged. "I don't think it's that he doesn't believe in the idea, it's more he doesn't want to expand right *now*. He wants me to be in Australia. He's suddenly started talking about retirement. Which is just ludicrous, the man's only fifty-five."

The corner of Bekka's mouth pulled into a half-smile. "Maybe he wants a break?"

"I don't know. Every time I ask, I just get a blank wall. I love the business, I always have, but I've never not been honest about wanting to put my mark on it. Expanding into the states is exactly that mark." He gritted his teeth, "I want that chance before agreeing to running the entire business."

"You seem different." Bekka murmured after a while. "Settled, and less arrogant."

"Less arrogant? I wasn't aware I'd ever been arrogant." He smiled.

"Oh yeah, you were many sorts of arrogant. You walked around campus like God's gift to women, with all the answers already in your back pocket. I hated your know-it-all attitude." She offered a meek laugh. "I'm big enough to now admit that maybe some of it was jealousy. Your life was so ideal. And you and Connor just hit it off so well, I kind of hated that you stepped into a friendship with him so easily, like you were taking his time away from me. Which is so silly now that I think about it."

Noah's chest ached. How little Bekka knew about his feelings towards her back then. Her confession just now explained so much about her attitude towards him. He'd never considered that she'd feel jealous of his friendship with Connor, he'd been too focused on blocking any feelings of attraction towards her. It made him feel even worse about having to have been the one to deliver her the news of Connor calling off the wedding.

"Bekka… I really am sorry about Connor. I tried to call you, after, but you changed your number and answered none of the emails I sent."

Her shoulder lifted in a slight shrug. "I couldn't stand to talk to you. At first, I just fell apart. Then after running into Connor, I let myself blame you more. It was the easy option. Easier than taking a step back and seeing that I'd been chasing a silly dream. I can see now I was more in love with the idea of being in love than actually experiencing it anymore. Connor and I had drifted apart. I just didn't want to see the signs."

The clutch in Noah's chest tightened further. "Were you being serious the other day when you said you'd given up on love?"

Bekka sucked in a deep breath, then shrugged. "Yes. It's just not in my genetic makeup. I think I need to accept that and move on."

It was too soon to push for more than friendship but Noah couldn't let her walk away from love without trying to change her mind. He tugged on her hand, walking towards the pier. The wood was a little tired at the edges but was solid underfoot. Smooch sniffed at the sides, though Noah noticed that Bekka held on tightly, stopping the dog from getting into the water.

"Bekka, you are a wedding dress designer. You are one of the most talented and creative people I know. You have an enormous heart and I can't see why you'd think finding love isn't part of your genetic makeup. That's just silly."

"Really? You're calling me silly?" she let out a short laugh.

He raised a brow at her. "No. I'm saying your thought process is silly."

"Well, it's okay for you, isn't it? Coming from the perfect family, with parents that love each other and provide a stable and supportive environment. Siblings you love and can lean on." Bitterness edged every clipped word.

Noah whooshed out a breath. "That's a lot of angst you've been building up in that head of yours. Would you like me to apologize for having a loving family? I know it was only ever you and your mom, but you never wanted to talk about your family."

Bekka tried to tug her hand away, but Noah gripped it tighter. "Please don't hide from me, Bekka."

Her eyes found his, hers full of confusion and hurt. "Why are you being so nice to me now? Is it pity? Five years later, you're back so you thought you'd try to atone for your friend's behavior?"

Still with the flinging of angry words, hoping to hurt if he was any judge of character. She could fling all she wanted, it wouldn't change how he felt. "I'm not walking away. This is not pity, or atonement. I told Connor exactly what I thought of his behavior. I tried to be honest with you Bekka, you knew early on that I thought you and Connor were too different. After you got engaged, I tried to point out that I saw cracks forming, but you never wanted to hear anything I said. I have only ever tried to offer you my total honesty and be your friend. Why are you still pushing me away?"

Her shoulders slumped like the last puffs of air leaving a balloon. This time when she tugged at her hand, he let it go. She scooped Smooch up, cuddling him against her chest. "I never met my dad. He did a runner the moment my mom told him she was pregnant. I grew up seeing my mom date a different man every other month, each one she claimed was 'the one'. *This time Bekka, this time it's the real deal.* And then she'd marry him only to fall apart when it didn't work out." Her voice was sour.

"That must have been hard."

"It was. And I vowed that I would only ever settle for the truest of love. The sort that brings you to your knees just hearing their name. Did Connor ever tell you I turned him down for a full year before I finally agreed to a date with him?"

Noah reeled on the inside at that tidbit of information. From the moment he'd met both Bekka and Connor, it had always been Bekka who had seemed more invested. The news that it hadn't always been the case came as a surprise.

"No. He didn't tell me that. He just said you'd been together since seventh grade."

Bekka twisted the leash in her hands, occasionally tugging Smooch back from whatever doggy smells he was finding. "We were friends before that. I'd known him for ages, and after he'd spent all that time without wavering in his feelings, never asking another girl out on a date, I thought maybe I could chance it. Then as each year passed, my mother would date another handful of men, marry one only to divorce, and I grew in my confidence with Connor. Maybe he was the one. That makes me sound a little crazy, doesn't it?"

Something within Noah's chest turned over. Was it any wonder that she was now disillusioned by love?

"No, it doesn't. Your mother was your complete family, your role model. You reacted how you needed to. The heart is a funny thing."

"It sure is." Bekka sighed and shook her head. "By college, Connor and I had been together so long I guess I had just blocked out any of the cracks. I'm a big enough girl now to tell you that the things you pointed out were correct. I just refused to see them. I was holding on so tight to my dreams, my stupid rule about just having one proper love and not being like my mother, that I wouldn't let anything else sway me. Connor and I wanted different things. He wanted to see the world, to travel. I wanted to start my tiny wedding business, get married, and then start a family. I had only thought to stay in New York to be with Connor."

"I never thought your design business was silly. It was like you were just marking time until you married Connor, which frustrated me, because you had, and still have, so much talent. I thought you were selling yourself short. Because I knew whenever I said my genuine feelings you got your hackles up, I figured if I offended you it would rile you up into action instead."

She pushed his arm. "Are you serious? They say women are complicated, but you take the cake. That even makes some convoluted sense, which annoys me no end."

Noah reached out and ran a hand down Bekka's arm, feeling slight goose bumps appear. "I'm sorry about your mom. No child deserves to grow up with a rotation of role models."

"She loves me, in her own way. I guess what I see now, is that she's searching for her happiness through a man. Which, incidentally, was what I ended up doing with Connor. I based every life choice about what he was doing, and that was exactly what I didn't want to be doing." She scoffed. "I tried to be nothing like my mother and ended up doing essentially the same thing. Anyway. Now I know where I went wrong and I will not be changing that for any man. I'm an official member of the No Brides Club and I'm taking my vows *very* seriously." She cemented her statement with a nod.

"So what exactly are those vows again?"

"Well… we're a group of strong, successful women who are focusing on our careers. We're putting ourselves first. No men need apply."

Noah wanted to bang his head against a wall. "But you're in the wedding business. You're surrounded by brides all day long. Are you honestly telling me you don't want that anymore?" Horror rang through his tone. His heart may have taken a serious dent the day she'd turned up to class sporting a solitaire diamond on her ring finger, put there by his own good friend, but he couldn't deny that her glow was pure gorgeousness. She'd been lit from within when she'd spoken about the engagement and their ideas for the wedding. Connor had been disinterested, a fact which had worried Noah greatly, especially when his friend had only just been talking about breaking up with Bekka.

He didn't want to believe that she'd given up all hopes of happily ever after in her future. Especially as every moment he spent with her made him want to be the man in that picture. He wanted to give their future a chance, but he couldn't do that if she'd crossed all possibilities off her list.

"I'm telling you no, I don't want that anymore." Her tone was solid, her gaze focused on the water. He leaned forward, hoping to capture her gaze, but she refused to look his way.

Well. If that's the case, then I'll just have to work even harder to change her mind.

"Righto. Well, since you don't believe in love and romance anymore, you're the perfect candidate for accompanying me on a horse-drawn carriage ride at dusk through Central Park."

Her face spun to his, her features incredulous. "How do you work that out?"

"Simple. If I take you, there's no chance you'll fall hopelessly in love with me. If I take any other girl, I couldn't possibly claim she wouldn't get the wrong idea."

"Scrap my earlier comments on your arrogance having dimmed." She laughed as Smooch licked her cheek. "You could go by yourself?"

"No way. That would waste a perfect opportunity. Besides, you're my unofficial helper in all things Valerie Fox wedding related."

"I have enough on my plate, but thank you for considering me for the position." Her eyes glinted with mirth.

"Come on, Bekka. You wouldn't leave a poor man hanging, would you? I'll look lost, and lonely, and desolate. Passersby will cry at the sadness emanating from my broken heart."

"You missed your calling."

"Please?"

"Oh my gosh, fine! If only to make you stop talking such nonsense."

She huffed, but he didn't miss the satisfied, brief smile that crossed her features. Bekka Arden might claim membership to some inane no man's club, but he had no intention of allowing her to stay involved. He just had to prove to her she'd already met the man of her dreams. Him.

CHAPTER 8

The sight and smell of horses had always made Bekka feel just a little scared and creeped out. They were enormous and their hooves looked like they'd hurt worse than putting a sewing machine needle through your finger. Something she'd herself done. Not a pain she ever wanted to re-live.

"You know, you will have to come a little closer to be able to climb into the carriage." Noah's voice was dry with just a touch of humor around the edges.

"Haha. You're funny." Bekka replied, but her voice caught. She swallowed to remove the giant lump that was forming in her throat.

"Hey, everything okay?" Noah bent at the knees, squinting into her eyes, which were hiding behind her favorite Prada sunglasses. A present to herself the first time her business had made it back into the black.

"Yep. I, uh, just hadn't factored in how big the horses would be."

Noah stepped closer, his hand finding hers with eerie precision. He'd held her hand a lot the prior day, causing tingles to hang around long after he'd dropped her home. A problem, to be sure. There was one thing that Bekka knew, and that was having any tingles for Noah would not end well.

"Bekka, they have to pull a carriage. See this," his free hand circled the large and ornate vehicle, complete with white rose's climbing around the sides, "this is the carriage. It's large and heavy. Like a car."

He appeared to be holding onto a laugh which escaped when she poked him in the belly. "No need to be sarcastic. I understand they would not be Shetland ponies. I guess I'd just forgotten how big a horse was."

Noah shook his head. "Come on, Cinderella, your carriage awaits."

"You better not be my prince charming." Bekka blurted.

"Why not? I'm very charming."

"No. You're wily. Like a Fox."

"You didn't." He gasped in horror.

Bekka grinned, enjoying this banter immensely. Noah had always hated being compared to any fox characteristics. A hangover from his childhood, apparently.

The step up into the carriage was high, and before she could take a breath Noah had scooped her up into his arms and deposited her onto the ledge of the open door. Air rushed into her mouth on a gasp. "Uh, thanks."

"You're very welcome," he said, sliding in close beside her. "This is the closed cabin carriage. There's another that Emilia has booked for us to try after that's open air."

"Valerie's in expert hands with Emilia. Whatever she wants, she'll get."

"You know Emilia well, then?" Noah remarked, conversationally.

"Yes, she's part of the club."

"Wait. But Valerie said she's happily married?"

"So?"

"So the club isn't like a lifelong commitment?"

"You are way more interested in this club than you should be." Bekka chuckled. "But since you ask, no. Quite a few of the girls have found their happy ever after."

"So there's hope for you, still."

Bekka shook her head, concentrating on the view out the window instead of giving Noah her attention and encouraging his line of conversation. "Why are you so interested in my love life? What about yours?"

"I thought you'd never ask." He fake sighed. "Alas, mine is rather slim on the ground. I'm enjoying hanging out with you though."

Bekka stilled, unsure if she should link those two comments and come up with two or was that making the wrong judgment? Did Noah mean that hanging out with her was part of his love life? Was he interested in her? Why did that scatter her thoughts in a million different directions and make her heart bounce with joy?

"Bekka?"

She spun to him, a smile plastered in place. "I'm really enjoying rebuilding a friendship with you too. I can see why you and Connor hit it off so well now."

Was it her imagination or did a frown cross Noah's face?

The carriage jolted, then started a slow meander forward. Bekka hadn't been paying attention to the fact they hadn't even moved yet.

Why had she put off Noah and taken the easy road? Even if he had been hinting at an interest in her, it didn't matter. Noah Fox was well outside her league, and besides, he lived on the other side of the world. Just because he was back for a short time now didn't make any difference. He was her ex's best friend and one of the last people she could see herself falling for her. Even if their bickering days appeared to have fallen behind them.

"Do you know you mutter under your breath when you're thinking?"

"I do not!"

"You kind of do. But no mind, I won't repeat anything I hear." He chuckled.

Bekka hated her treacherous body for enjoying that

sound. She gathered her courage and changed the subject. "How is Connor doing?"

Noah shifted next to her, his thigh bumping against hers. His tone changed, losing the lightness it had held until now. "Do you really want to talk about Connor?"

"Yes."

Noah sighed. "He's good, working in San Francisco. He said he was hoping to catch up while I'm here in the states. We don't talk as often as we used to. I'm pretty annoyed with him to be honest, after what you told me he said."

"Don't be. I've come to terms with Connor and me not being right for each other. It took me a while, but I can see that it was the right thing for us to break up. Even if his method of doing so still smarts. I don't want to be a thorn in your friendship."

"You're too forgiving," Noah muttered.

"Have you spoken to your father after seeing the property?" Bekka might have used discussion of Connor to help shield her heart from progressing any further along the Noah street, but that didn't mean she wanted to focus on him either.

Noah sighed. "I sent him pictures. We had a conference call late last night, but he wasn't very enthusiastic. The call circled back around to me taking over the business and him retiring. We ended the conversation on another argument. I just don't get it." Frustration emanated from Noah as he shifted in his seat.

"Maybe your dad is tired of working?"

Noah scoffed. "My dad is a lot of things, but he's not tired of working. He visits every single site once a month, more often if he can swing it. He's forever micromanaging each of the hotel's managers. A fact I know as I've often had to smooth over their ruffled feathers afterward. My mother's wanted to go on a cruise to Vancouver and up to Alaska for heaven knows how long. At the beginning of the year, they started booking flights and had a stack of brochures and now Dad's canceled that because he wants to focus on supposedly teaching me everything I don't know about the business."

"Is there anything you don't know?" Bekka gave him a wry smile, trying to lighten the dark tone that was shadowing his features.

"That's just it—no! Unless dad has run the business into the ground or bought a stack of other locations unbeknownst to anyone, then I can't see anything else I would need to learn. But that aside, he's so focused on the business. He'd be bored in minutes if he gave it up."

"You mentioned your mom's broken ankle, maybe that's it? Or having Valerie's wedding? Maybe he wants to lock you into the business before you find true love and gallop off overseas like your sister?"

He pinned her with his piercing gaze. "Finding love overseas wouldn't stop me from being part of the business."

Bekka swallowed, unable to ignore the obvious undercurrent to that statement. She broke away, focusing out the window as trees and shrubbery rattled past. It was an enchanting experience riding around at near dusk in a carriage, especially when accompanied by a handsome man. Valerie would love this. It fit perfectly with the wedding she'd described so far.

Noah cleared his throat. "Maybe mom's ankle has thrown dad. His change in attitude came around that time."

"Have you asked him?" Bekka inquired, turning back to him. Noah's fingers inched across the space and played with hers, sending soft tingles up and down her bare arms. She wished she'd brought a jacket. As though she'd spoken, Noah shrugged out of his jacket and swept it around her shoulders, cocooning her in his recent warmth which only sent more chills down her spine.

"When I asked, he said mom's fall had made him think of his father who had died soon after a fall. Dad was left, unprepared, with the business and hadn't coped well." He frowned.

"That explanation fits with your dad's sudden push for you to take over. Would taking the top job be so bad?"

"No. It's just not what I want for now. I want to focus on something else." His gaze sought hers and held.

Bekka stilled, the air shifting as new currents flowed between them. Noah shifted closer, leaned in a little, his body language clear. Her body ached to follow suit, but her head screamed no. Noah would kiss her. She sensed it, knew it within her bones like she knew when a design was finally perfect. Her eyes fluttered, Noah's lips so close she could feel his breath hot against her mouth.

The carriage jolted and Bekka turned her head, scrunching her eyes tight. She heard an almost silent muttered curse but steadfastly kept her gaze out the window, pretending she hadn't just run from kissing Noah Fox's very tempting mouth.

Bekka's phone chimed in her purse, and she pulled it out to read the incoming text, welcoming the distraction.

'Tom and I are getting married! Isn't that wonderful, darling? This is it for me, the real deal, I just know it. Mom x.'

Each word she read placed another stone on the border around her heart. Another reminder of why it was better she not become romantically involved with Noah.

"Well, look at that. My mother's getting married again." Her words were bitter.

"Again? What happened to the last guy?"

"They divorced two years ago. This one she's been dating a whole two months."

"Are you okay?" Noah's hand reached out to her, his fingers grasping hers with a gentle squeeze, but she pulled her hand away, tucking it into her lap. She was glad he didn't mention trying to kiss her.

"Of course. What's another wedding. Another father figure who won't last."

"Maybe this time it will."

She turned her head, taking in Noah's hopeful expression. It was easy for him to always look on the bright side with love, but from her side of the fence, it always ended the same.

"Maybe." She offered, hoping that would close the conversation.

"You know you're not your mother." Noah breathed.

"I know that. I can't even get a guy to the altar."

She stared out the tiny window of the carriage, regretting her words and berating herself for checking her phone. Her evening had been going just fine until her mother had texted with her latest love quest. It just felt like another slap in the face.

"I think perhaps you're not as fine with the Connor situation as you said." Noah pushed, an edge to his words.

"Look, let's just set aside any talk of Connor or my mother. I'm flabbergasted at her persistence with this quest of hers to find the perfect man. It's been going on my entire life and I'm now twenty-eight. You'd think by now she'd just give in and admit that there's no such thing as a perfect man."

"Well now, that's not true. You're discounting me." He held his palms out and winked. Bekka rolled her eyes but was secretly warmed by his attempt to lighten the mood. She was taking her pain and frustration around her mother out on Noah which wasn't right. Even after she'd just avoided kissing him, he was still trying to lighten her mood.

He reached out to take her hand, and this time she let him. The connection was welcome. Returning her gaze to the window, she took in the glittering trees as dusk fell. While she knew she wouldn't ever be using a carriage for her own wedding, and hadn't ever wanted to, she had to admit that it was wonderfully romantic.

"I think Valerie should opt for this closed in carriage. It might be warm during the day, but the air will become cool and her dress is strapless. Do you mind if I leave after this ride? I really need to get back to my work."

Noah squeezed her hand. "Sure. I'll ask the driver to turn us around."

Her friend Devon glided onto the stool opposite Bekka's at their favorite milkshake bar. Bekka had already ordered chocolate for herself, strawberry for Chelsea who was yet to arrive and vanilla for Devon. It had become a tradition for them, though neither Bekka nor Devon had been as free to catch up regularly now that Devon was officially with Sven and Bekka's workload had skyrocketed.

"You look like you've got a lot on your mind, sweetie."

Bekka smiled, loving the southern drawl of her friend. It was so cozy and warm. "Just busy with work."

"So, nothing to do with the tall, dark, and tasty man Chelsea mentioned seeing at your studio?"

"No, nothing to do with Noah."

Chelsea chose that moment to arrive, popping up onto the seat and taking a giant slurp of her strawberry shake. "It's definitely something to do with Noah."

Bekka focused on her straw. The pink and white striped paper was already starting to fall apart from her chewing on one end. "Okay. Fine. It's to do with Noah."

"Finally!" Chelsea grinned. "So what's the deal with you two? You spent most of the weekend together."

"He's only here for his sister's wedding, and some business stuff. He's not here permanently."

"So?"

"So… any feelings I *may* develop are destined to go nowhere."

"That's progress, at least you're admitting feelings now." Devon slotted in, a cheeky grin lighting her face.

Chelsea swiped at a ginger curl that had sprung loose from her messy top knot. "Bekka, you need to stop judging everything by your past."

"I'm not." She retorted quickly.

"You are, sugar." Devon and Chelsea exchanged looks. "Every guy you've dated you've barely given them one date before coming up with an excuse why it won't work. You can't shield yourself from love. Just because things didn't work with Connor."

Bekka sighed. "It's not only that. My mom's engaged. Again."

Chelsea's brows shot up. "Didn't you tell me recently she only just get divorced?"

"Yep. The ink's barely dried on those papers and already she's leaping headfirst into her next marriage. Supposedly this one's *The One*." Bekka pulled her straw out, licking the end, and then popped it on a napkin. "Let's say I give in to these feelings, which I'm pretty sure Noah is reciprocating: how can it go anywhere? My life is here in New York, his is in Australia."

"Do you have to have a long-term outlook sorted before you've even gone on a date?" Chelsea scrunched her nose, as though the idea confused her greatly.

Bekka looked at Devon, then back at Chelsea. "I can't have my heart broken again. After Connor... my business went up in smoke and I'd barely started. My business is so much more now, I don't know if I'd survive another shattered heart."

"And what if Noah's the one, Bekka? Are you saying you're not even going to try? Think of everything you could walk away from."

Picking up her glass she drained the last of her shake, the chocolate milk cool and soothing against her throat which was tight. Did she want to take that risk? Something inside her told her that maybe Noah would be worth it. Every time she was in his company, it was easy to forget her reasons for not wanting to fall in love again. Ever since she'd turned from his kiss, she'd struggled to think of how it would have felt.

What if Noah was her soul mate? Could she have her cake and eat it too?

Bekka was thrown when Noah turned up early Monday morning in jogging gear with two takeaway coffee cups in hand. She didn't want to know how he'd found out her favorite order, but gave in to his offer of accompanying her and Smooch for a walk. After taking her normal route, Noah walked both her and Smooch back to her front door with the promise of seeing her again the next day.

She was left standing there with a silly grin on her face, a whimpering puppy at her feet as Noah left.

True to his word, he returned at the same time the following day, and the day after that. By Friday it had become second nature to expect him to be waiting on her doorstep at eight a.m., coffee's in hand.

"I was thinking we should go to that Italian place for dinner," Noah spoke casually, as though not wanting to startle her.

Instead of allowing herself to prevaricate, she just jumped in. "Okay. Sure, that would be lovely. When works for you?"

"How's tonight?"

"Tonight? But tonight's date night."

"I didn't think you were dating."

"I'm not. But surely you have better things to do than spend your Friday evening taking me to dinner?"

"Nope. In fact, it would be my absolute honor."

Smooch yipped and ran around in a little circle. Worried about another scampering episode, Bekka clutched the leash nice and tight, hiding her face, which she knew was going pink.

"I, uh, have a confession too that you may not like," Noah said sheepishly.

"Okay, let me have it?"

"I've ordered some cabinets. For your workroom."

Bekka frowned. "Why?"

"Well, I noticed some of your fabrics were getting dust on them and you were muttering yesterday that you couldn't find those beading samples. I was at the shops with Valerie, she's redoing her living room, and well they were there and just looked perfect." He stumbled over his words and the uncertainty on his face gave her a little ping inside.

"Oh, Noah. You're waiting for me to blow up, aren't you?"

"Maybe. A little. Are you mad? I can cancel the order if you really don't want them, but I think they'll make a vast difference. They are white with nice clean lines, a selection of three matching that will fit across the wall. Added shelving space and the last if we don't put shelves in you can stand your fabrics up in there which will shelter them from dust."

Bekka leaned in and kissed Noah on the cheek. "Thank you. That's really thoughtful."

Bekka couldn't help feeling smug at causing color to brighten his cheeks. "I'll install them this weekend. If that suits?"

"Sure. My friend's coming over tomorrow afternoon to go through the photoshoot images, but other than that I'll be in my workroom finishing your sister's dress for her fitting next week."

"Can I see it?"

"What? The dress?"

"Yeah. I'm interested in what you do, how you make your designs come to life."

"Okay, sure." Noah taking an interest in her work made her gooey inside.

The thought of having a date night dinner with Noah also sent flutters bouncing around. Maybe her friends were right, and she needed to just give this a chance instead of finding reasons it will all go wrong. Noah had mentioned he'd be around a lot more if the hotel plans went ahead, which he seemed very positive about. It was time she showed herself that she'd shed her past instead of just telling everyone she had.

Bekka signed the delivery card with a flourish, giving the piece of paper a quick flap to help the ink dry before she attached it to the box that was sitting, waiting for collection by a client.

Noah turned to Bekka. "Why is your name spelled with two K's? I've always wondered."

She sighed. "Good question. I asked my mom once, and she just laughed and said wasn't it more fun having the name Bekka spelled differently to everyone else. I can't say I agree, since I've had a lifetime of having to spell it out for others or ask for certificates to be reprinted due to spelling errors."

"If you don't like it, why don't you just change it?"

"I suppose I could. But no matter how much it grates on me, it's also a reminder of how far I've come. How different my life is now compared to the sad, lonely, poor kid whose mom couldn't be bothered to give her the same level of love that she so freely bestowed on whatever man was passing through our life."

Silence met her words and eventually she turned to see Noah just standing there, staring at her aghast.

"Was it really that bad?" he asked with a deep frown between his expressive eyes.

"Not always, no. But most of the time. I learned early on to be self-sufficient and take care of myself. When Mom broke up with her latest guy—which always happened—she'd fall in a heap and need me to take care of her as well. I suppose, in hindsight, that's why I'm still smarting over Connor. It's not the breakup, so much as my realizing how dependent I'd become on him. You were right, though I didn't want to see it. I was changing my life goals and plans to fit with his. I'd become my mother."

Noah scoffed. "That's taking it too far. You were starry-eyed for him, yes, but you were still your own person. It sounds like your mother doesn't retain much of herself when she becomes involved with a man. Have you ever spoken to her about it?"

"No."

What would she even say to her mother? Thanks for never being present during my childhood? No. She shook her head as if to emphasize her thoughts. There was no point. Besides, she'd moved on now. Her life was solid, she had her business. She was rebuilding a friendship with Noah. So maybe she found him just a little more attractive than she should… that didn't mean she had to do anything about it. They could casually date and see where it went. Noah didn't understand that sometimes family issues needed to just stay in the past. Talking to her mother wouldn't change anything.

CHAPTER 9

*N*oah straightened his tie, swallowing back nerves before he knocked on the pale blue front door of Bekka's shop. She'd told him to come through the front since she'd most likely be doing some finishing touches on Valerie's dress. The door swung open and Noah lost the ability to breathe.

Bekka was a vision.

Pale gold silk wrapped around her slim figure, showcasing every last inch. Her feet were bare, her toenails painted a light pink that matched her finger-nails. Her face shone with fresh-faced beauty and minimal makeup. He ached to lean in and place a kiss against her lips but after his last botched effort, didn't dare try again just yet.

"Hi," She said, cocking her head to the side in query.

"Hi! Sorry! You look amazing." He stammered.

Her cheeks flushed, and she ducked her head down.

"Thanks. Come in. I'm nearly done, just let me finish a bit of stitching and then find my shoes."

He followed her through, expecting her to be in her workroom, but she had set herself up in the fitting room. Center stage was a gown on a mannequin that he knew would make Valerie scream with delight.

"Wowsers. That's a lot of fabric."

"It is, isn't it? I'll see if your sister wants to tone it down a little, but hopefully, she'll be happy with the finished product."

"I know she will be. You are one talented lady."

"Thanks." She smiled. "Have a seat."

He took the offer, folding his frame into the plush blue sofa. It looked so delicate, but he was pleasantly surprised when it enveloped his frame with comfort.

"You've chosen well with this place. The high ceilings really add to the natural light and give a relaxed vibe. I imagine a lot of bridal studios could feel quite stressful at times."

"I suppose. I worked in a few to gain experience before I found my feet enough to start my own business. The Soho location I was looking at was twice as big as this place, but this felt right for now. I plan to expand one day. My main ethos is ensuring the bride gets what she wants and walks out of here with nothing but one hundred and ten percent satisfaction and a pleasant experience."

Noah nodded, looking about the space. This room

had a thick pile carpet which squished underfoot. The walls were quite a stark white, and he figured that helped to not detract attention from whatever dress the bride was trying on. The front showroom had polished oak floors and a softer feel to it. This room was more serious. The one exception to this room was the over the top crystal chandelier that hung above the fitting stand.

"That's quite the glittery piece," he commented, nodding to the roof.

Bekka's gaze followed, and she grinned. "That was a personal extravagance, I've always wanted a chandelier coated with crystals. It's just so glamorous and iconic for wedding finery."

"It is that." He hooked a foot over one knee, enjoying watching Bekka as she worked.

"How are the plans for your new hotel coming along?" Bekka asked, her attention solely on the dress before her. As he watched, she pulled a few pins from a bracelet at her wrist, sticking them in varying spots around the top of the dress. He did not understand what she was doing, but it was taking all of her concentration.

"They are on track for now. I sent some final plans and sketches to my father yesterday. Clark has checked my costings. The seller has promised me another two weeks before they will officially put it on the market. So I just need to get all my ducks in a row and get Dad's final approval."

"What will you do if he says no?" her eyes flicked to his, concern in their depths.

"I'll buy it, anyway."

"Really?"

"Yep. I'll beg my bank manager to extend me the extra credit I need and I'll go out on my own."

"Isn't that risky?"

"Possibly. But if you don't take a chance, you never know… right?"

He'd hoped his words would elicit a grin, but her gaze became shuttered and she focused back on her work.

"Is Smooch in your apartment? I might go say hi while you finish up."

"Just go straight through. I'll only be another minute. Sorry about the delay."

"No problem," Noah murmured. He walked past, picking up hints of her delicate floral fragrance. He wanted to drink it in, in fact, he wanted to step close to her and envelop her in his arms, but he didn't dare. He still had some work to do with breaking down the barriers that Bekka had up. He just needed time to do so, he was sure of it.

It wasn't long before Bekka came through the door, a satisfied smile in place.

"I'll just grab my shoes."

Noah was sitting at her kitchen counter, Smooch happily laid out before him as he gave the dog tummy rubs. "No problem. All done?" he called after her figure that retreated into a darkened room behind the kitchen.

"As done as can be until the fitting with your sister. Then I'm sure there will be more changes. Three weeks to go though, so it should all be fine." Bekka returned to the room and slipped her feet into a pair of black skyscraper heels.

"You look like you could do serious damage with those." He joked.

A grin split her face. "These are my power—don't mess with me—heels."

"You name your heels?"

"Of course. They all have their special uses."

"Forget I asked."

"I'm sure Valerie has the same."

Living in his sister's apartment and having seen her shoe collection, he had to agree with her there.

Walking into the Italian restaurant with Bekka at his side left Noah feeling euphoric. They were shown to an intimate table for two at the back corner of the dining area and left to peruse the menu.

"Shall we order a bottle of wine or would you prefer water or just a cocktail?"

"Let's split a bottle. The food here is delicious, and the servings generous. We may be a while."

Sounds perfect to me, Noah thought.

After placing their orders, Noah leaned in, collecting up Bekka's hand that lay on the white tablecloth. It felt so natural and relaxed to be here with her. They talked about his business and ideas for the Long Island hotel until his phone ringing interrupted them. He excused himself and went outside to take the call.

"Hey Mom, what's up?"

"Have you spoken to your father?" she rushed out.

"No. Well, not recently. I sent him the final ideas for the new hotel yesterday but haven't heard back from him. Why? Is something the matter?" his mother sounded weird.

"No, no. Nothing's the matter. I just hoped he'd spoken to you by now."

"About what?"

Silence stretched and Noah's heartbeat pulsed. "Mom, what is going on?"

"Nothing, sweetheart. I saw the plans, you've done some excellent work but I'm not sure this is the right time to be expanding into another country."

Noah's brows raised, a heaviness settling over his chest. "I thought you were on board with this idea?"

"I am, sweetheart. I think expansion into America is a good move for us, particularly the East Coast, but not right now."

"That's quite an about change. You've been so supportive of this venture." Noah fired back, unease causing a harsh tone to his voice.

"I am supportive. Look, I shouldn't have mentioned

anything. Can you please try to call your father in the morning?"

Huffing out a breath, Noah agreed and hung up. His mother was hinting at some issue but refused to tell him. What on earth was going on that would change his mother's support? And what did his father need to tell him? Questions without answers swirled in his mind, leaving him with nothing but a dull headache.

Bekka took a sip of the fruity cabernet as she waited for Noah to return. She'd second-guessed her decision to have dinner every three seconds since she'd agreed to the date, but so far it had done nothing but over-deliver on her expectations. Noah was so easy to be around. The conversation was flowing and she need not have worried they'd have nothing to discuss.

It made her wonder how much of their friendship she'd ruined back in college with her attitude. Her behavior really did have a lot to answer for. Thinking back to that time it made her cringe to see how easily she'd fallen into a love for Connor that she'd liken to her mother's. She'd been so desperate to not act like her mom, and yet, she'd ended up loving a man in the same way. To the point she'd ignored his faults, she'd ignored the cracks that in hindsight were so obvious. What would have happened if Connor *had* gone through with the wedding? Would she have given up more of her dreams to suit him? Would she have become even more of a shadow of herself just to please him?

That path of thinking caused her stomach to take a deep dive, and she grabbed for her drink, taking a large gulp. There was no doubt in her mind that love was dangerous. She didn't want to take that risk again, which meant she had to tread lightly with Noah. He was sweet, funny, and charming and far too handsome for his own good. He was a real liability to her chained up heart.

He returned a short while later and took his seat, Bekka noticed immediately that something distracted him, a frown marring his face.

"What's wrong?"

"Nothing. Well, no, not nothing. My mom called, but she was being very odd."

"What did she want?"

"That's just it. She called to see if I'd spoken to my dad. When I said I hadn't heard from him she clammed up. Now I don't know what to think."

"Do you think something's happened? Should you call Valerie?"

"Maybe," Noah muttered, his gaze focused outside the glass windows beside their table.

The waiter placed their entrees on the table, interrupting the conversation. Bekka looked at the enormous plate of carbonara and wondered how she'd make even a dent. Being left with her thoughts for those few minutes had killed her appetite.

It appeared Noah's had also diminished. She watched as he shifted his marinara pasta around on his plate, taking just one bite and chewing it for ages.

Bekka put her fork down, deciding this was pointless. "Go call Valerie."

"I'll call her later. I don't want to interrupt our meal."

"I think we can both safely say we're distracted and concerned." She looked pointedly at his meal and her own, both looking untouched after sitting there for at least five minutes.

"Are you sure?"

"Please. I'm worrying now too."

Noah placed his navy linen napkin on the table and took his phone back outside.

Bekka toyed with her pasta, forcing another mouthful in. The salty flavor of bacon was offset perfectly with caramelized cream, the al dente pasta had just the right bite, and yet it may as well have been cardboard. Letting her fork slump against the plate, she picked up her own napkin and started folding it into a flower, if only to keep her fingers busy.

Another minute passed, and Bekka wondered if they should just call it a night. Noah returned, a grimace on his face.

"I'm sorry. I got through to Valerie, eventually. She

spoke to Dad earlier today, and she said he was fine, she thinks it's probably something to do with the wedding and maybe she had a point." Bekka could see that Noah was still distracted, his eyes barely meeting hers.

He dug into his meal, which by now was probably cold. Bekka made herself eat another few forkfuls before she gave up, her tummy swirling in knots. She placed her hand on the table where it had been when Noah had taken it earlier, but he didn't notice.

The mood was well and truly broken. Should Bekka take that as a sign?

Bekka woke the following morning and took Smooch out for an early walk. After dinner last night, Noah had walked her back to her front door, giving her a light kiss on the cheek, promising to see her later the following day. She assumed that meant he wouldn't be there for his morning dog walk activity that had become their thing over the past week.

She'd tossed and turned most of the night, unable to settle.

Was she imagining Noah's interest? Had she been so wrapped up in their date before his phone call that she'd just romanticized the whole night up to that point? Surely not. He had tried to kiss her last weekend, she'd have put money on it.

Hating her thoughts and cursing her stupidity with

dating, she gave herself a stern talking to. It was time to refocus. Her business was thriving and with Valerie's dress and the additional activities with Noah, she was falling behind on her schedule. She needed to get her act together with pattern-making her new collection and sourcing the fabrics and trims. There was a stack of beading samples on her desk she hadn't even looked at, and fabric swatches from a new distributor. She'd planned to look into some print designs, exclusive ones, and she hadn't even touched on those details. Plus, she needed to refit the Smithson dress as Cathy had lost a drastic five pounds in the past month.

She'd allowed herself to be well and truly distracted, but no more. She had a fitting this morning, and then she'd knock over some of those other tasks. Chelsea would be by to visit too, so at least she'd have some company to keep her thoughts away from a certain guy.

The morning passed in a blur as she didn't even notice the time until the bell on her shop chimed well after lunch. Rubbing her eyes, she pulled the door in and stared blankly at a delivery man.

"I've got a delivery for Bekka Arden?"

Bekka blinked. "Right. Yes, that's me." She poked her head around the burly man's torso to take in the collection of long boxes. "What are they?"

He consulted his list. "Says here they are cabinets."

"Oh! Sorry, of course. My mind was elsewhere." Not that she'd forgotten about Noah and his gift, but she thought he'd arrive with them in person. She harrumphed, unsure where to put them. "I guess you must put them in the front room here. They are quite big."

She stepped back and allowed the guy to drag in each box until her entry was all but blocked.

Signing the slip for delivery, she waved off the truck. She'd only taken three steps back towards her workroom when the bell rang again. She dropped her head back and glared at her ceiling. This was not getting her work done.

This time Noah stood on her doorstep, a delighted smile in place. "Sorry, I was held up talking to my dad. Seems he and Mom were just having a difference of opinion on the expansion and got their wires crossed, but it's all sorted now. I'm so, so sorry about dinner last night."

Seeing Noah, her heart flipped. "Don't be. It was a long week, and they worried you. I completely understand." Which was the truth, even if her own feelings were less easy to decipher.

"Can I make it up to you with an offer of another dinner date?"

She chuckled and stepped aside so he could come in. "That's not necessary."

"Maybe not. But I'd like a chance to improve. I'm having dinner with Valerie tonight, she's bringing Arnold so I can finally meet him. I'd love it if you could come with me."

That smile. She bet he'd get away with anything if he shined that megawatt grin around. She knew before the word left her mouth she'd agree to anything he asked.

"Okay."

"Yeah?"

She didn't think it was possible, but his face lit up even more. So much for her decision to just focus on work. "Yes! Now can you please install these cabinets?"

He grabbed her by the waist and lifting her high, he spun her around before depositing her back to the floor, completely dazzled and giddy.

"Your wish is my command." He winked before getting to work.

Bekka wandered back to her workroom, trying to ignore the galloping horses that were thundering about inside her chest.

Wind whistled past the open window above the desk Noah had commandeered in his sister's apartment. Standing, he pulled it closed, enjoying the blissful silence. Valerie was due back in about half an hour, and then they'd be heading straight for dinner. He just wanted to get a few details completed before she got back. Plus, it seemed a good way to distract himself from the energy coursing through him at the prospect of spending another evening in Bekka's company.

Noah stretched, his muscles sore from his foray into cabinet installing earlier. It had taken longer than he'd expected, but had been worth every moment he'd been able to spend with Bekka.

He loved watching her work, her brows drawn in concentration, her slight mutters as ideas came and went.

Her love and joy for designing was forefront whenever he'd glanced her way.

Chelsea, her friend, had been delightful, and he hadn't missed the surreptitious thumbs up and wink she'd thrown Bekka's way when she'd thought he wasn't looking. Having her friend on his side could only be a bonus.

His cell phone buzzed, breaking him from his thoughts. Searching on the desk, he unearthed it from under some blueprints.

"Noah speaking." He answered.

"Noah! It's Connor, man. How are you?"

His friend sounded ecstatic and Noah realized he had promised to call Connor earlier in the week, but the thought had completely blanked from his mind.

"I'm good." He swallowed uneasily. Should he tell Connor that he and Bekka were sort of seeing each other? He hadn't yet worked up the courage to kiss Bekka, especially after his previous botched attempt, but he planned to. As soon as he could see she was ready.

"I have news." Connor continued, seemingly oblivious to Noah's pause.

"Yeah?"

"I'm engaged, man. She said yes!" Connor's laugh guffawed down the phone line, each yip of happiness grating against Noah's nerves and sending a sinking feeling to the pit of his stomach.

"Engaged? I didn't know you were seeing anyone."

"Remember, I told you about Tiffany? She's a waitress. We met two years ago when I was traveling around Europe. Anyway, she's home in San Fran and we reconnected recently. Man, she's such a babe. I'm the luckiest man alive."

Noah wanted to hit something. Connor had been the luckiest man alive when he'd been with Bekka, and he'd treated her like dirt.

"Uh, congratulations." He said through gritted teeth.

"Try to rein in that enthusiasm."

Noah let out a huff. "To be brutally honest, I'm still frustrated with you. I cannot believe you told Bekka that your breakup with her was all my fault."

"I thought we'd moved past this? Ancient history, remember?"

"Well, maybe I'm not past it. I've been spending a bit of time with Bekka. She deserved better than what you put her through."

Silence met his words. "Spending time with her, how?"

"Just hanging out." Noah retorted.

Connor made a dismissive noise. "You're still into her, aren't you?"

Noah jolted. Connor had known? "Look, I'll lay it down straight. I like Bekka. Yes, I had a thing for her back in college—which I did nothing about—I swear."

Now it was Connor's turn to sigh. "Yeah, I know. I think knowing you had a thing for her, made me hold on to my relationship with her tighter. I always envied you, man. She was the one thing I felt I had that you didn't."

Noah didn't know what to say to that. All he could do was wish they'd been able to have these open conversations earlier, without five years having passed. Five years where Bekka had despised him and built up a total resistance to wanting to date anyone. If he'd known he could have helped her, he could have been there for her.

"Look, Noah. I know you aren't happy with how I ended things with Bekka. I will call her, and apologize, it's long overdue. I just wasn't ready for the relationship she seemed to want. We'd been together for years and I guess I just took the coward's way out."

"You do need to call her and apologize. But don't tell her about your engagement. Please. Let me do it?"

Connor made a noise that may have been an agreement or possibly a harrumph. "How serious are you two?"

"I'm serious enough about her to not want to see

her hurt. I'm giving her time and space to see that I'm the perfect guy for her."

Connor laughed. "Well man, if she can't see that, then she's not the Bekka I used to know. I'm happy for you, truly."

"I'm happy for you, too. I'm looking forward to meeting Tiffany."

Noah hung up, feeling the heaviness lifted from his shoulders. He'd always felt like there'd been a barrier in his friendship with Connor after he'd called off the wedding. It seemed there had been. But now it felt like the path had been cleared. Connor knew that he had feelings for Bekka and planned to act on them. Now he just needed to break the news to Bekka about Connor's engagement and hope it didn't send her spiraling away from the progress they'd made.

CHAPTER 10

*V*alerie threw her arms around Noah, placing kisses on both sides of his face.

"Hey big brother. Come meet Arnie."

"Do you really call him Arnie?"

"Well. Not to his face." She replied impishly. "Bekka, you look utterly stunning!" Valerie continued, turning to Bekka, who stood beside him.

Noah had his arm clamped around her waist, holding her close to his side. He couldn't help himself. She was dressed in a sleek black dress that shimmered whenever she moved. It was simple, but on her, it looked like a million dollars. He'd been seriously impressed when she'd admitted to having made it herself, though by now he should be used to her endless talent.

"Doesn't she?" Noah inserted as Valerie leaned in to kiss Bekka's cheek. "She made the dress herself."

Bekka blushed. "Ignore your brother. It's so good to see you. How was San Francisco?"

"So lovely. I got to see Arnold for over three minutes in a row, daily! I love, love, love the photos you've sent of the dress. I can't wait to try it on next week."

Valerie scooted over to Noah's other side, hooking her arm through his. "Arnold's already at the table."

They weaved their way through the restaurant, Noah ushering both women before him. Reaching the table they were greeted by a tall guy with reddish blonde hair. His face shone with a goofy grin, his eyes focused solely on Valerie. That was all Noah needed to know to like Arnold.

"Arnold, this is my brother, Noah and his… friend, Bekka Arden. Who also happens to be my brilliant wedding dress designer."

Noah couldn't help but notice his sister's slight hesitation over her use of the term 'friend'. Pushing the thought aside to discuss with her later he shook the hand offered. "Nice to meet you."

"Finally." Arnold said, his laugh a little deprecating. "I'm sorry I wasn't able to catch you last year when we went to Sydney."

Valerie rolled her eyes. "Noah's spent the past few years updating everything within each of our hotels and dragging our systems into the current century. We might have had the name already established but Noah's out to take it even higher."

Heat spread across the back of his neck, added by the fact that Bekka shifted a little closer to accept Arnold's handshake. He slipped a casual arm about her waist and pulled her into his side. She smelled like pure heaven.

"Oh, I forgot to tell you!" Valerie's high pitched voice interrupted his musing. "We ran into Connor while in San Fran and I invited him to the wedding."

Bekka stiffened within his embrace.

Noah glanced at her and then back to his sister. "You invited Connor to your wedding? Connor Chivers? When did that happen?"

"Yeah. I ran into him at the airport before our flight this morning. I met him when you were in college together and I came to visit, remember?"

"Yes. I remember. I just didn't realize you would have, and that you'd invite him to your wedding. Valerie, this event is becoming bigger than Ben Hur. You need to rein it in."

Noah panicked. He needed to get Bekka alone to tell her about Connor. Would he have told Valerie about his own engagement? Why the heck hadn't Connor mentioned Valerie had invited him to the wedding when they'd spoken earlier that afternoon.

"Ooookay. I thought you'd be happy? He's your mate, isn't he?"

Noah glanced quickly at Bekka. Her facial expression hadn't changed, well not to the normal eye. To an experienced eye, one that had spent every second studying her for the past few weeks, there was a slight pinch firing between her brows. One that spoke of stress, and a situation unknown.

"Yes. We're friends. Val, can you excuse us for a minute? I need to speak to Bekka alone."

"Oh. Okay. But don't be long, we should order before it gets busy." His sister stammered, her face a picture of confusion as Noah corralled Bekka back the way they'd come and outside of the restaurant.

He turned her so she faced him. "Talk to me."

"About what?"

"Um, how about we start with the bombshell my sister just dropped on us? I didn't, in a million years, think she'd invite Connor to the wedding."

"It's fine, Noah. He's your friend. She was doing what she thought was right."

"You're my friend too."

"Yes."

"So you're cool with this? You'll still come?"

Her eyes closed as she dragged in a breath. From that one moment, he knew to prepare for a battle.

"Look, Noah. Your sister doesn't really know me, and as lovely as it was for her to invite me… I think it's probably best all around, if I don't—"

"Decline?" he inserted.

"Noah…"

"No. Do not *Noah* me. That's reserved for my mother, and only my mother. I want *you* to be there. If you change your mind on coming because Connor will now be there, then I'll call him right now and rescind his invitation."

Bekka's eyes widened. "You'd do that?"

"If seeing him there will make you uncomfortable. Yes."

"Oh."

"So?"

Her eyes flicked to his, then fluttered away. "That's quite a lot to take in Noah. You and Connor are good friends."

"Yes, but you mean more to me than that."

Her eyes slammed shut, and he worried he'd pushed too hard. Taking a step closer, he ran a finger down the side of her hand. Slowly, steady, just a subtle touch to show her he was there. It was like dealing with a startled deer. He was desperate for her not to flee.

"Bekka, you are more important to me," he whispered.

His words hung in the air. Her eyes slowly blinked open and found his. "Really?"

"Yes. Really. Truly."

Her breath whooshed out. "Okay. Then I guess I'll be there."

"I need to add something."

The deer in headlights look came straight back to the forefront. But no way would he not be one hundred percent honest with her.

"I spoke to Connor this afternoon. He's engaged." He blurted.

She shifted her hand away, folding her arms across her chest. "Engaged?"

"Yes." He confirmed.

"I see." Her mouth thinned. "How long?"

"I don't know how long he's been engaged. I only just found out."

"Hopefully he sticks this time."

He could see she wanted to add more, but stopped herself.

"Bekka don't do this. Don't shut me out, please?"

"I'm not. I appreciate you telling me. It's better that I found out now and not be blindsided at the wedding with all those people around. It's fine. I don't have feelings for Connor anymore."

"That doesn't mean it wouldn't still hurt to hear he's engaged to someone else after what happened. I was thinking… you could come as my partner."

Her wide eyes flung to his. The words hung like an explosion of tart raspberry amongst chocolate mousse cake.

"Your partner? Like a date?" she clarified.

"Yes. We could say we're dating. If you want. If that helps."

Give him strength. He was making such a hash of this. He had wanted to ask her properly. Not this obscure offer of shelter. He was such a wimp. Connor's announcement had thrown him. As much as he wanted to believe her words that she was well past what had happened, he wasn't sure she was.

"It's fine. I don't need shelter, Noah. I'm a big girl now, I can handle seeing my ex and his new… girlfriend. Fiancée, even."

"Bekka. I know you. I can see this has thrown you for six. I don't want to see you hurting again because of me, and you coming to the wedding is just as much for me as it is for Valerie. I never wanted to be the one to hurt you, but it feels like I'm always the one ending up in that position."

She reached out, placing a hand to his chest. "Oh, Noah. You're such a good guy. Connor doesn't deserve you as a friend."

"I'm not doing this for Connor." His tone must have signaled a change, because her eyes flew to his. "I'm doing this for you. Surely how I feel about you is obvious by now?"

Her mouth formed a cute little 'O' and before he could let himself think twice he stepped in and took those lips with his own. He'd expected her lips to feel soft as clouds and twice as heavenly, but they over-delivered. Kissing Bekka felt like everything and tasted better than light-as-air cake coated in whipped chocolate ganache.

And he loved ganache.

He allowed himself to savor the moment. Tracing the outline of her plush mouth with his own, pushing and pulling, her kissing him back with every second that passed. With one last dash of his lips against hers, he stepped back.

"You kissed me." She shot out.

"Yes."

"Why?" Her eyes flicked to his, latching on accusingly.

"I'd think that was obvious, Bekka. I like you. I more than like you. I see a connection here, one I've always felt from the moment we met. Even when you were with Connor, I tried to block it out but couldn't. I had thought after years of not seeing you that the feelings would have diminished, but they came back threefold the moment I laid eyes on you, twirling in front of the mirror. The ball is in your court. I'm laying all my cards on the table here, I want to be more. But if you want to remain just friends then that's all we'll be."

"And if I don't want that?" she said, from under her lashes that darted faster than a hummingbird.

"We'll play this however you want to."

"Okay." She said and smiled a beautiful smile that shone brighter than the sun rising over the ocean.

A part of Noah clunked into place. He'd come here to pursue dreams not yet taken, which was turning out far better than he could have ever hoped. The vendor had confirmed yesterday that his offer was verbally accepted—the paperwork just needed finalizing—which took care of his head and his career. Today he'd gambled his heart and won. Bekka now knew of his feelings and was ready to give him a chance.

Life could only get better from here.

Bekka floated on a cloud the whole of the next day. Dinner had been delightful, but all Bekka could focus on were the thoughts of Noah having kissed her. He held her hand the whole evening and had kissed her again when he'd dropped her home. It had started slow and sweet, progressing to a deeper embrace. His tenderness and reading of her had shifted a few more of the blocks around her heart.

Could she do this? Could she take a chance on Noah?

He'd said he'd had feelings for her for years.

That revelation had shocked her, especially as she'd always thought Noah barely tolerated her back then.

How bad was she at reading people?

She shooed away the unwelcome thought.

He'd asked to see her again today, but Bekka had to decline. The work really was piling up and as much as she wanted to give in and just spend time with him, she knew she couldn't let herself fall too hard and fast. This was a time to take things slowly.

Chelsea arrived just before lunch, coffees and bagels in hand.

"Hey lady, sorry we didn't finish going through the photos yesterday," she said in greeting.

"That's not your fault, it's mine. I'm the one who should say sorry that you had to come back again today."

"I'm always happy to hang out in your shop. Besides, I want more information about last night's date! Noah was looking all sorts of fine when he was installing those cabinets yesterday. You're welcome to send him over to fix my studio whenever you want."

Bekka gave her friend a droll look. "You don't let anyone in your studio."

"Oh yeah. Details." She shrugged. "So?"

"He kissed me." Bekka blurted, unable to keep the information to herself anymore.

"You go, lady! How was it? I bet he's an amazing kisser."

Her cheeks flamed red. "I'm in trouble, Chelsea. It was good. Superb."

"Why is that trouble?"

"Because… what if I fall for him?"

"Then you can get married, live happily ever after, and make gorgeous babies."

She flicked a look at Chelsea. "Be serious. He's based on the other side of the world."

"Does that really matter? And is that really what's stopping you?"

"I don't know. It doesn't when we're together. But when I'm away from him, I take a step back and all I can see are the obstacles between us. I'm worried."

"Is this still about Connor?"

"No. Actually, Noah told me he's engaged, and will be at his sister's wedding. Which I'll also be at. I thought I'd freak out, and initially I did, but now... it's not that. That's not what's holding me back."

"Then what is?"

"I'm not sure."

"Then perhaps you can agree to just let things take their natural course? Try not to run from something that is this good. I was watching Noah yesterday. He could barely take his eyes off you, honey. He's smitten. And I have an eye for reading people. That's what makes me a fantastic photographer."

Bekka reached out and hugged her friend. "Thank you. Now let's look at these photos. Let's go through to the kitchen so Smooch doesn't tear a hole in the door."

Plus looking at photos would hopefully take her mind of reliving Noah's kisses for more than five seconds.

Noah glanced over the last of the plans, then gathered them up and slid them into a folder. There were still a few weeks until the wedding and if he had his way, he wouldn't be returning to Sydney afterward.

He'd spoken to the vendor again on Friday and had confirmed another viewing of the location so he could do a video call with his father. Even though his offer was accepted, his dad was lagging on giving the final go-ahead on the location being part of the Luxury Fox Group. He hadn't been lying when he'd told Bekka that he'd walk away from the company and start his own if his father didn't get on board with this expansion. The memory of his mother's call poked its way into his head again, but he brushed it aside. When he'd spoken to his dad he had laughed at his wife's worrywart ways, saying that mom had misunderstood what he'd said. Noah had pushed, but his dad had been adamant that it was nothing.

Would his father agree to the deal?

He had a few other locations to look at, but none were as perfect as this one. None gave him everything he needed on the one spot, with little renovations required.

Besides, he wanted to be in town to spend time with Bekka. It was so freeing to have finally admitted his feelings for her. He'd seen the shock on her face when he'd told her his connection to her went back to their time at college. It was clear she hadn't been expecting that, but he was going all in. He wanted her to know that his feelings were solid and that they wouldn't be changing soon.

He picked up the phone to send Bekka a text, requesting she meet him at four-thirty a.m. tomorrow.

Her initial response was negative, but when he promised decadent, and delicious delights she relented. Who could say no to fresh-baked pastries and cake?

A full night's sleep under his belt, Noah knocked at the powder blue door of Bekka's studio at exactly four-thirty the next morning. He waited a few minutes before knocking again.

A light switched on and he heard a few bumps and a soft grumble before the door swung inwards.

"I don't like you," Bekka said with a huff.

Noah grinned. She looked adorable. Her hair was all mussed, her cheeks pink from sleep. She did an enormous yawn and rubbed at her eyes before returning to her slumped posture and accusatory glare.

"You agreed to this." Noah quipped, a brow raised, not at all phased by the grumbling beauty before him.

"I must have been insane." She rolled her eyes before letting go of the door handle and walking away from him. He followed close behind.

"Is there coffee with these to-die-for pastries?" Not waiting for a response, she muttered, "there better be coffee."

Noah looked around, expecting Smooch to come bounding towards him.

"There will be coffee. Where's Smooch?" he offered conversationally.

"Asleep. Where all normal functioning beings are."

"You have five minutes," Noah said with a grin.

"Did I mention I hate you?"

"Yep." His grin spread wider.

Ten minutes and a change later, they were in Noah's rental car and driving through the Tribeca streets towards Brooklyn. Bekka was clutching the takeaway coffee he'd brought for her like it was a lifeline.

"If you'd told me there was coffee in the car, I'd have moved quicker."

"Duly noted for next time."

She gawked at him. "I can assure you there won't be a next time. I don't do this time of morning. Ever."

"Then I feel privileged. You may change your mind after tasting these pastries, though."

Bekka muttered something unintelligible under her breath, which Noah ignored.

There was light traffic about, but nothing like it would be later on. Pierre had given Noah the tip about this pastry shop, run by a friend of his. Given his penchant for all things sweet, Noah couldn't miss the opportunity. Pierre had informed him to arrive early to avoid disappointment.

"This must be it," Noah said, pulling into a park. Across the road, he could see a small crowd out the front of a window stall.

Bekka cocked her head. "Wow. Who are these crazy people desperate for sugar at this time of day?"

Noah chuckled. "C'mon sleepyhead. I'll make you eat your words."

Ten minutes later, they sat on a park bench that looked back towards the Brooklyn Bridge, a small mountain of pastries between them. Noah took his first bite of an almond croissant, the flaky pastry melting as his taste buds sang.

"Oh my god, try this," Bekka said in awe. Her eyes were closed and a blissful expression floated across her features as she chewed slowly. "This is the best thing I have ever tasted."

"That's the apple pie, yeah?"

"I don't know. It's just sweet, delicious, and addictive." Bekka took another bite, moaning this time.

Noah shifted at the sound. She held out the pie for him and he took a bite, hit with the strong flavors of succulent apple and cinnamon encased in light as air pastry.

"Here, try this." He held out his croissant and watched as she chomped off one end, chewing thoughtfully then shaking her head.

"I like mine better, but it's a close call. I have to hand it to you, Fox. This was well worth the early morning."

Seeing her grin with delight and dive back into the pastry made the trip worthwhile for him. Heck, just seeing her made it worth it.

Reaching over, he swiped a thumb across the corner of her mouth where a tiny flake of pastry sat. He popped it in his mouth, sucking the sugar off. Every moment he spent with Bekka made him more sure that she was the one for him. Now all he had to do was convince her to take another shot at love. With him.

CHAPTER 11

*B*ekka yawned as she walked through from her workroom into the kitchen to make coffee. Her outing with Noah this morning had been worth it for the delectable food—and company—but her mind was now paying the price. She'd planned to have an early night to counteract the early morning she knew she'd have, but had become lost in designing some new dresses last night. Her planned eight p.m. bedtime had become midnight.

Added to that when her head had finally hit the pillow, sleep hadn't come. She'd tossed and turned, unable to block out thoughts of Noah's lips and just where this thing between them could go. Just thinking of his kisses now sent her knees weak and her stomach swooping to the ground. *You've got it bad, girl.*

Stifling another yawn, she poured black coffee into a tall mug. Instead of going back to her desk, she took the coffee through to her bedroom and relaxed on the bed next to Smooch. Her dog half lifted an eye, as though glaring at her for interrupting his rest, and then resettled a little closer to her leg.

A few sips of the fiery liquid had her feeling more relaxed than alert, so she placed the mug on her bedside table, worried she'd end up spilling it all over herself.

Snuggling against Smooch, Bekka figured closing her eyes for a bit couldn't hurt.

She came to with a start.

The sky outside was drifting towards dark. It hadn't been dark when she'd come in? Panic-stricken, Bekka lurched from her reclined position and grabbed at the clock beside the bed. *Oh no.* It was after three in the afternoon.

I fell asleep. For three hours!

Racing out of her bedroom, she sprinted to her desk, a sick churning in her stomach.

Rifling through papers, she searched for her appointment book. Why is my life such a mess? This year was meant to be the time she got everything worked out. From a financial point of view, she was almost there at the goal she'd set, but in terms of her actual life, it felt more chaotic than ever.

Am I over-reacting with Noah being back?

Spying the diary under a stack of wedding magazines, she pulled it out and quickly flicked to the marked page. *Briony Smith—3:20 p.m.* Oh no! Dumping the appointment book, Bekka dashed back through to her bedroom. She looked a complete mess! Tussled and fuzzy hair from her unplanned nap. No makeup. Dressed in sweats. This was a disaster!

Why had she allowed herself to fall asleep?

More to the point, why had she allowed herself to be talked into a crazy early morning date when she had so much going on with work?

Enough. She could work out the answers to those questions another time. Right now she had to make herself presentable and professional in less than ten minutes.

Noah took the seat across from his sister at the cafe around the corner from her apartment in Soho.

"I've already ordered. You'll need to go tell them what you want." Valerie said in greeting.

"Already done. How's the wedding prep?" he asked, noting the folder that sat on the table before his sister, filled with paper, one of Bekka's sketches peeking from the corner.

"Great! Emilia is so organized. And I really appreciated those tasks I could leave with you. Within the month I'll have my dream wedding with my dream man."

"I'm glad to hear it's all coming together."

"Hmm." Valerie nodded, finally shifting her focus

from her phone screen. The waiter came out and placed their coffees before them. His sister's hazel eyes tracked his movements as he picked up the espresso and took a small sip.

"Hmm?" he queried.

"Just how involved are you and Bekka?"

He put the cup back down, concerned about the look his sister was sporting.

"I like her, a lot. And I believe she's starting to develop feelings for me too. Why do you ask?"

"You're really distracted, Noah. And I've barely seen you. I'm excited for you, I am. But Bekka's business is very much ingrained within the New York bridal scene. Dad mentioned to me yesterday that he offered the reins of the business to you and you haven't given him an answer. Is Bekka the reason?"

Noah huffed. He loved his family with all his heart, but sometimes having such a close-knit one meant they subjected him to conversations he'd rather avoid.

"Yes, and no. I've always had a thing for Bekka, from the time I met her in college years ago. I had thought after returning to Australia for a few years that those feelings would have dwindled, but they didn't. I still thought of her constantly. I kept track of her career, and well when you announced your engagement I knew I had to come out here."

"Right, so spending time with me was just a smokescreen." Valerie poked her tongue out at him.

"You know that's not the case." He grinned back.

"But it was the kick I needed. Seeing her… something inside clicked back into place. I've never felt this way about a woman, Valerie. She makes the air seem cleaner, the sky brighter… she's never tried to be anyone else with me."

"And Connor?"

"He knows. He's happy for me."

"And what about the business?"

That was where Noah stumbled inside. He still hadn't worked out a solution to that particular problem, nor had he discussed it with Bekka. He wanted to, so much. He wanted to be honest and lay his life goals and plans on the table for her, but worried that it would send her tumbling away from him. Besides. Taking over the company just wasn't something he saw himself doing at age thirty-one.

"Why is Dad suddenly so keen to hand over the reins? Did he say anything to you?"

"No. Just that he thought he and Mom should go travel before they get old." Valerie rolled her eyes dramatically. "If you ask me, he's going through a mid-life crisis, Dad style. I think I'd prefer the red sports car option personally, but you know Dad. It's always about family and Mom."

Noah sighed, sitting back in his chair. "Yeah. He's definitely all about the family. I think that's why I feel so bad. Like not being ready now is letting him down. I just figured I'd spend more time seeing what I could add to the business before taking over the top helm."

Valerie sipped at her coffee, then replaced the cup onto the saucer with a small chink. Her gaze leveled on him, a brow raised expectantly. "So?"

"So what?"

"So what are you planning to add to the business? It wouldn't be a hotel based in Long Island by any chance?"

Noah startled. "How did you hear that?"

"Um, duh. Arnold. He has his fingers on everything! Why haven't you said anything to me? I've been waiting for a message to come visit the place at least."

A smile spread across Valerie's face, which was all the encouragement Noah needed. "Name the time you're free and I'll call the seller to arrange it."

"It's a direct sale then?"

"No, it's through an agent still. But I've been speaking directly to the seller about certain aspects, and it's been easier to go direct for site visits. They are aware of my ideas. I've got the new plans back at the apartment if you want to look them over? The place will be amazing. Smaller than most of the Australian ones, but top quality."

"You've really thought this through."

"Absolutely. Dad would have it no less."

"So, he's on board?"

"Getting there. We're in a mutual considering phase."

"Right. He's considering the expansion into America, and you're considering taking the leadership role of Fox Luxury?"

"Yep."

She scrunched her nose, wiggled it a little like a rabbit before a slight look of concern took over.

"How does Bekka feature in all of that if you take the job?"

I don't know.

Noah opened his mouth to say just that and then shut it. "I'll find a way. There's always a way."

Unfortunately, his sister's face spoke of all the uncertainty that rocketed about inside him. What if there was no way to have his cake and eat it too?

The next morning dawned bright and full of sunshine. Bekka brewed coffee and went straight to her desk to work before promising Smooch a mid-morning walk later in the day. She secretly hoped that Noah would turn up to accompany them, but also didn't want to allow the wish to blossom too wide.

The client had been five minutes late yesterday—thank goodness—and Bekka had only felt slightly breathless and out of her element. She'd always prided herself on being on time and precise and well prepared for a client meeting. The clients made her business, and the bridal business was small. Poor service could make or break her future, and no way did she want to feel that terrible loss and lack of direction again.

Connor's breaking off the wedding had hurt, desperately so, but it had been nothing to the realization of how much she'd messed up with her fledgling business. The past years had been nothing but hard work and gritty determination to get back her reputation. Yesterday had been a wakeup call, that she needed to make sure her head was properly in the game and on her work. Noah was… Noah. And a huge distraction.

Unfortunately, she was honest enough with herself to know that telling him they could only be friends just wasn't an option anymore.

Which meant she had to be extra careful. No way would she allow herself to fall head over heels in love. For now, this had to stay light. Fun. She could do light and fun.

Having given herself that stern talking to, she got back to work.

Except her mind kept wandering.

Flicking her wrist up, she realized it was already past nine. Should she just take Smooch for his walk, anyway? *No. I'll give it another half an hour.*

Three attempts at sketches later, she gave up, and instead, figured she'd do the work physically. Sometimes free-form drapery gave her better results when she was feeling on edge. Valerie's dress was in its last stages and only needed to be fitted tomorrow, but as it was such a show stopper and a big name wedding, it had left a gap in her next collection. It wasn't complete now. The design Valerie had chosen incorporated too much of one of her major designs that she scrapped it and wanted to put in something new.

The only issue was that she couldn't quite get it right on paper. The idea was there, lurking in the depths of her mind, but she just couldn't pull it out. It was eluding her, which was driving her slightly mental.

Dragging her mannequin from its new hiding place in her cabinets—which looked awesome—she positioned it in the middle. Her eyes floated back to the cabinets. Grabbing her phone before she could rethink the interruption, she texted Noah a thank-you message. She'd thanked him profusely after he'd installed them, but the realization right now of how much she needed them made her want to acknowledge him once more.

She cut a few large rectangles of white voile, then starting pinning it into place. The voile was soft and malleable for shaping, a perfect and cheaper substitute for silk. Perhaps that's what she was missing from this design? Was the fabric right?

Picking up a pen from her desk, she tapped it against her lips for a moment before drawing some lines on the fabric. Time floated as she pleated, pinned, unpinned, and drew various lines until she had a rough bodice shape that she was happy with. With a satisfied nod, she stepped back. Not perfect—yet—but much closer than what she was getting to on the page.

Sometimes that was just how it worked for her.

Humming a little, she picked up her phone and congratulated herself that she'd gone an entire half an hour without thinking about Noah.

There was a reply waiting from him, a little smiley emoticon. Her heart dropped a little with disappointment that he hadn't reached out or suggested they catch up.

Oh gosh, lady. You've got it bad already.

Refusing to ponder that any further, she placed the phone on her desk and walked over to open the door to her living area. She whistled for Smooch, who came padding out of her bedroom.

"Shall we go for a walk buddy? Who needs a man when I have you."

Smooch sat and cocked his head, as though ready to listen.

"Walk?" Bekka repeated, unhooking the leash which elicited a little enthusiasm in the small dog.

Bekka closed up, then at the last minute changed her mind and raced back in to get her phone quickly. She could check a few emails and update her to-do list while she walked. Multi-tasking was healthy.

The sun was hotter than she'd expected, which had her going back inside to grab a hat.

Finally feeling ready, Bekka walked to the front of her path. Instead of going left, she turned right. *Change is as good as a holiday, right?*

Smooch yipped and turned in a circle, looking back

the way they'd normally go. Tugging on the leash, he did his doggy version of a sigh and then started trotting along in front of Bekka.

See, she could do things differently. Take chances. She was a successful business owner, thrilled and satisfied with her life. She had a handsome man she was semi dating.

The thought made her tummy wobble.

Should she tell the No Brides Club that she was kind of seeing someone? It's not like it hadn't happened with others... some members were now happily married or in serious relationships. The indecision threw her.

Previously, she wouldn't have thought twice about admitting to having a date or having noticed a cute man somewhere. She was still a woman, even if she was choosing to put her career first right now.

But Noah was a different kettle of fish.

Everything about Noah screamed warning bells for her heart.

As if she'd conjured him, her phone beeped with a message, his name flashing on her screen.

Hey Bekka, sorry I couldn't swing past for our daily Smooch walk. I'm showing Valerie the site. Are you free for lunch later?

She should say no. She had a mountain of work to finalize, plus she wanted to finish draping her latest design. Pulling up her to-do list she added a few more things. There was a fabric order on there that she needed to place today or she'd miss the cutoff to receive her shipment in line with her schedule, but she could do that tonight. Nothing on the list was super urgent. There were no appointments for today.

She shook her body, wriggling off the excitement that had sprouted wings and was flying through her veins. She should really say no.

Her traitorous fingers typed out yes. A grin a mile wide spread across her face.

Suddenly, she couldn't wait for lunchtime to roll around.

The car's flowed in a gentle pattern, like ants gliding around before rain. From his high up viewpoint in Valerie's apartment, Noah sat at the window and peeled a piece of an orange segment before popping it into his mouth.

Lunch with Bekka had been delightful yesterday, even though he'd talked her into staying well past when he should have. They'd collected Smooch and gone for a walk around Central Park, lost in the crowd, just two lucky souls holding hands.

He hadn't spent a lot of time just sitting back and relaxing in the past few years. He'd been working hard, learning everything he could about the business, making improvements where he thought he could. But now, here... he realized how isolated he'd made himself. Sure, he'd gone out with friends from back home and gone on a few dates, but he'd not connected in a way that he was with Bekka.

Had he been in a holding pattern? That made him feel ridiculous.

It also put a lot more pressure on whatever answer he gave his dad with the business.

A few times yesterday he'd gone to bring up his dilemma but had chickened out at the last moment. If he told Bekka he was thinking of taking over the company, would she end things between them? When they'd only just reached this point? He desperately hoped not. He was still hoping some divine idea would pop into his head that allowed everyone to be happy and get what they wanted.

Unfortunately, he just couldn't see that happening without one of them sacrificing—big time. It was too early to think like that. He'd only just kissed her, finally, this past weekend. Springing on her the idea of maybe moving to Australia? No.

He had time. There were still a few weeks until the wedding. Maybe he could negotiate with his father for more time. Surely he could put off retirement for another few years, one at the very least?

Bekka lifted the veil up and left it to float down over Valerie's face. The dress fit perfectly, with only a few minor adjustments being required. Bekka silently thanked the fashion gods for that good luck. It didn't always happen with brides, since often they were so emotional their weights could fluctuate between fittings, but Valerie was nothing but calm, her figure appearing unchanged from when she'd taken her measurements.

"Okay, you can turn around now," Bekka said.

Valerie spun, her hands flying to her mouth as she gasped. "Oh. Oh! Bekka! It's… amazing."

The delight that shone on the other woman's face was all the thanks Bekka required, and that moment was exactly what kept Bekka in this game. Pulling out her phone, she snapped a few pictures. Valerie twirled, the gigantic tulle skirt layers floating back into place.

"Do you want to look at these? If there are any you want, I'll email them to you. I just thought you might like to show your mom."

Valerie did one last twirl before the mirror before clasping her hands and jumping with excitement. "Oh yes, Mom will love seeing them. Thank you for thinking of that! I can't believe I didn't think to do so."

Bekka nodded, then asked the question that had plagued her since Valerie had arrived. "Weren't any of your bridesmaid's free?"

"Oh, probably. But I wanted to do this alone." She laughed. "Seems silly, I'm sure, but I wanted my mom here and well, because she couldn't be, I kind of didn't want anyone else seeing the dress until she had. Does that make sense?"

Bekka's heart skipped at the beautiful sentiment. She felt for Valerie. Having had a lifetime of wishing for a mother who cared more, who put half of the effort into her daughter as she did her relationships, she knew what it felt like to wish. Except in this instance, Valerie had the perfect mother. The only reason she wasn't here was because she'd hurt her leg.

"It does. Here, I can take a video of you on your phone if you like? Then you can send it now."

"Oh, gosh, would you mind? Thank you." Valerie enthused, handing over the phone.

Bekka pressed play and enjoyed the moment as Valerie spun and jumped and threw layers of her skirts into the air, all the while giggling delightedly. Handing the phone back, she went to the other room to jot down a few notes and give Valerie some privacy to send her message.

Returning, she was surprised to see Valerie had stepped down off the dais and was sitting in a giant pile of skirts.

"Did you want to see how the dress looks without the top layer?"

"In a minute. I just wanted to talk to you."

Now it was Bekka's turn for another surprise. "Oh okay. Is something the matter?" It wasn't unusual for brides to have emotional reactions to their dresses during fittings, needing to just talk through problems or ponder ideas. Bekka often felt a little like a priest, offering a carefully neutral listening ear.

"You and Noah are dating."

It was a statement, not a question, so Bekka just nodded. When the other woman just continued to stare at her for a bit Bekka felt she should say something. "Yes. We're dating. It's new though."

"But serious?"

Bekka laced her fingers together, then unlaced them. "I guess so."

"Noah said he'd told you of his crush from the moment you two met. He was pretty cut up about how your engagement with Connor ended when he returned to Australia. I was only there a short time before I returned here for work, but I saw how it hurt him. You two weren't even in a relationship, but seeing you hurt, hurt him a lot."

"It hurt me too."

"I know. I suppose I'm just trying to work out how serious you are about him. I know it's nosy and unprofessional, but Noah's my big brother. I love him to pieces, but with you, he's always had his heart on his sleeve. You have the power to hurt him in a way no one else ever has. If you asked him he'd move here to be with you."

Bekka was floored. Every muscle in her body tensed. "I don't think so." She countered. Sure, Noah had said he'd had a crush on her all those years ago, but this wasn't that serious. Yet. She knew it could get there... she knew already that her feelings were invested more than they should be. But Noah wasn't there already, was he? What Valerie was suggesting was a stretch.

"Look Bekka, whether or not you believe it, Noah's really serious about you. I just wanted you to know that. I hope you won't break his heart."

Bekka nodded, as though on autopilot. "I would never do anything to hurt Noah."

The moment she said the words, she knew them to be true. Which was equally thrilling and scary. Just how involved was she letting herself be in this relationship already?

Noah arrived to collect Valerie from her fitting. Partly to help his sister, but mostly because he wanted to see Bekka.

He pressed the doorbell and waited. Bekka answered after a few moments, a small smile spreading across those gorgeous features of hers.

"Hey. I was in the neighborhood. Figured I'd swing past and save Valerie the cab fare."

"Right." She said, pulling the door open wider.

He stepped inside, and then before he could stop himself he bent and kissed Bekka. She tasted better than chocolate cake.

"Hi," he murmured against her lips, nipping one last quick kiss.

"Hi, again." She giggled. That sound alone made the

trip worthwhile.

"Hey, you two lovebirds!" Valerie's voice interrupted his plans to dive in for a third kiss.

"Hey, sis. Nearly ready to go?"

"Yep, just finished. The dress is… out of this world divine."

Noah caught the blush the stole over Bekka's features before she ducked her head. "My pleasure."

"Actually while you're both here. Are you free tonight?" Valerie said.

Noah shrugged, his eyes finding Bekka's, a brow raised. They hadn't discussed doing anything, though Noah had planned to talk her into having dinner with him. He'd found another Italian restaurant that came highly recommended that he wanted to take her to.

"I should probably—"

Noah cut off Bekka. "You aren't going to say work, are you?"

"Actually. Yes." She arched her brows and skewered him with a pointed look.

"Work, schmerk. I need you both to come help me with wedding stuff." Valerie inserted.

Noah glanced over at his sister and immediately went on high alert. Her smile was far too devious. "What sort of wedding stuff?"

"Oh, never mind that. Just say you'll be there."

"Do we have a choice?" he countered.

"Nope." Valerie grinned. Walking forward, she gave Bekka a hug, pulling her in tight. A slight frown pulled Bekka's brows together before she returned the hug.

"C'mon brother. Let's let Bekka work her magic. We'll come collect you at six tonight."

Noah barely placed a kiss against Bekka's cheek before he was dragged back outside.

"Dance class," Noah repeated, a slight film of sweat popping up at the back of his spine.

"Yes! Won't it be fun?" Valerie clapped her hands together and then hugged Arnold.

As much as sticking pins in my eyes. Noah was happy to see that Arnold was also lacking enthusiasm for this activity and had a pained expression lurking in his gaze. He shot Noah a quick look, as though begging him to be on board.

"Uh, sure sis. So you're serious about the wedding party doing a dance then?"

"Of course! It will look brilliant. Bekka I know you're not in the bridal party but I really want you to feel included too."

Bekka squeezed his hand so hard he had to grit his teeth.

"What sort of dance class is it?" Bekka asked.

"Oh, it's a mixture. Come on, the others are already inside."

Noah threw Bekka an apologetic look, waiting until

his sister and Arnold were out of earshot. "I'm sorry about this. I'll talk to her if you really don't want to be included."

Bekka folded up her bottom lip, gently biting the soft flesh. "No. It's okay. It's actually really thoughtful of her to include me."

"So you'll do it?" Noah clarified.

"I will. I'm not going to miss out on the chance of watching you make a total fool of yourself for your sister. You get big brownie points for this."

"As in actual brownies?"

That earned him an eye roll.

Inside the dance hall, a few other women and men crowded around his sister. He really didn't want to go through with this, especially as he knew himself to have two left feet for dancing. A waltz he could probably have managed. But actual choreography that he'd have to memorize and practice? His body ached at the thought.

Five steps in, he knew he was in hell. Their dance teacher appeared to have limbs that bent in ways that left Noah convinced he wasn't human. Luckily, and to his intense surprise, he wasn't even the worst dancer of the group. One of Valerie's bridesmaids and one groomsman were worse. Noah gritted his teeth and mentally plotted revenge as he jumped, side-stepped and fist pumped with the best of them.

Bekka was dressed in activewear that made him want to personally thank the inventor of spandex. She had a natural rhythm that kept up with the teacher and left him envious. Standing behind her in the lineup was torturous, but he had to admit it was probably better than the reverse, which would have given her a front-row seat of just how bad he was.

"This is my version of hell." He whispered at her ear when they were awarded a drink break.

"Oh c'mon. It's kind of fun." She glanced over at Valerie who was laughing, wrapped up in Arnold's arms. "Your sister is having a ball."

"Yes, that makes this slightly more tolerable. You're a fantastic dancer."

Her already pink cheeks deepened. "You're a fantastic brother for agreeing to this. Most wouldn't."

"Well, you know what they say: real men dance!" He struck a pose he hoped would imitate the teacher. Unfortunately, it went south, and he ended up tripping over his feet and slumped onto the ground.

"Yup. I can see that." Bekka said with a snort.

Bekka hadn't laughed that hard in a long time. Her stomach muscles were already aching. Noah had dropped her home, his face red with shame and exertion from the dance class. She'd begged off on the offer of dinner, claiming that she really did have some admin work to catch up on.

Walking through the door, she gave Smooch a cuddle, before going through her usual routine of feeding and allowing the dog outside to do his doggy thing.

Deciding a cup of tea would help soothe some of her hyped-up nerves, she brewed a cup and carried it through to her workroom. Her desk was its usual quagmire of papers, so she set about tidying that before she tackled her to-do list.

She pulled out her appointment book, going through from the top and ticking off items or shifting them to a new list. She checked the fabric order from France, then froze. The pen hovered over that item, a sense of dread spreading through her chest. Had she placed that order? She'd needed to place it the other night, but now that she thought about it, she couldn't recall putting the order in.

Shoving the chair out, she raced over to her filing cabinet. Rifling through the papers, she checked her file twice but came up blank.

I haven't placed the order.

Her heart sunk, acid bubbling at the back of her now dry throat.

Taking careful steps back to her desk, she collected up her mobile phone and searched for the fabric distributor's number, praying that Amelie could work some sort of miracle.

The phone rang a few times before it connected. "Bekka! I've been expecting your call. How are you?"

"Frazzled. I have a huge favor to beg of you."

The other women's tinkling laughter sounded down the line. "Let me guess, you need me to put an order in for you that I should have had two days ago?"

Bekka let out her own deprecating laugh. "Yes. Please. I'll beg. Whatever it takes."

"Yes, yes. Email it to me now and I'll see if I can work my magic. I spoke to Frances yesterday, who was surprised she had received nothing from you. I think it quite hurt her thinking you'd gone elsewhere."

"No, where else does lace and embroidery work like they do? I'll just triple check the order and send it now. You are an angel."

"So who is he?"

Bekka froze. "Who is who?"

"The guy, darling. The one who has got you so tied up in knots that you're forgetting to place orders. That's really not like you. Or have I misread the happy I'm hearing in your voice. Well, under the panic that is."

Was it that obvious? Was that what this was? Her heartbeat trebled to the point she wondered if it would beat right out of her chest. With fingers that shook, she pulled up the order on her computer screen, buying some time while she worked out how on earth to respond.

"He must be something to have you distracted from work-related items. I'll look out for the wedding announcement." Amelie said, not noticing the deathly silence on the other end of the line.

"I've got the order, just emailing it now." Bekka blurted before hanging up.

Sugar! I'm in too deep. What on earth am I going to do now?

Shoving aside her inner turmoil screaming at her, she quickly scanned the list and double-checked it against her design sheets. Clicking send, she slumped back in her chair.

Was hanging out with Noah causing this distraction?

She was falling for him. Her eyes fluttered shut. *Oh, sweet lord, I'm falling for Noah Fox. What is wrong with me?*

CHAPTER 13

The Briarwood Tavern was bustling as Bekka carefully picked a path through the throng of Wall Street traders. She was late again and hoped the others hadn't waited for her to order their dinner in the restaurant. The noise thinned a little as she entered the dining room of the Tavern and spotted her friends over at their usual table.

"Bekka, you made it." Chelsea smiled in greeting.

She leaned in and gave the petite blonde a hug before proceeding around the table and completing similar greetings.

"Kinsley!" she squealed as she reached the elegant blonde at one end, "goodness it's been forever. I'm glad Dylan let you out of his sight to come visit."

Kinsley King was one of the original No Brides Club members, and a legend in real estate circles. Happily married now, she lived part-time in Camille at the Wildlife Sanctuary that had brought her together with her true love. It was always extra special when she made it to one of their meetings.

"Lovely to see you, Bekka. A little bird told me you've scored Valerie Fox as a client."

"That little birdy is correct." Bekka grinned, ignoring the wobble that reverberated through her at the mention of the word Fox. She took the empty seat between Chelsea and Kinsley. Marnie, Devon, and Emilia were deep in conversation across the table, though Emmy threw her a quick wink when she sat.

A cocktail glass was placed before her and she groaned when she took a sip of the sweet drink.

"Long day?" Kinsley remarked.

"Long week," Bekka replied. "Do you know much about the Long Island real estate market?"

"Enough to know it's pricey. Why do you ask?"

"A friend is interested in an estate there. They plan to turn it into a boutique hotel."

"A friend? That wouldn't be Noah Fox of the Luxury Fox Hotel group, would it?"

Bekka took a small gulp of her drink. "Yes. Do you know him?"

"No. But I heard he was looking at the place over the weekend. How do you know him? He's Australian isn't he?"

Chelsea leaned in, "Oh, he and Bekka go waaaay back. He's been taking her for walks every day this week and even talked her into a romantic carriage ride in Central Park."

Bekka's cheeks flamed, and she wondered if she could crawl under the table unnoticed. "It's not like that. We're… friends." *Liar, liar, pants on fire.*

"I wish my friends looked at me the way he looks at you." Chelsea quipped with a raised brow. "He's smitten."

"No. No, no, no. We went to college together. I'm helping his sister."

"So when I dropped the photos over the other day he wasn't sitting in your prized workroom, reorganizing your chaos and yards of tulle?"

Bekka made no pretense of not gulping her drink this time. "He wanted to help since I offered to take the carriage ride with him. He worried he'd look silly doing it alone. The carriage ride, I mean. Besides, it was for his sister who is a client."

"That's a lot of excuses you're making there, Bekka. Maybe you're up next on the register to fall off the club wagon and into love's arms." Kinsley said with a knowing smile.

"Noah didn't ask me to take the carriage ride with him, and I'm working with his sister too." Emilia piped up, her face a picture of loved up bliss.

Bekka just shook her head again, then excused herself to go order dinner and another drink. She'd spent the past twenty-four hours giving herself a very good talking to. Noah Fox was not a good idea. They were friends, that was all. She was not in the market for love, or turning her life upside down for a man. She'd thought she'd found her one genuine love once and look how that had turned out. She would not have her head turned again on a whim. In fact, her life was perfectly satisfactory without a man and she had no reason to change that. She would not become her mother.

Her friends were making a big deal out of nothing. She was in the No Brides Club for very valid reasons. Her career goals weren't met yet. Maybe in a few years, she might be ready to dip back into the dating pool.

Noah's green eyes flashed into her mind, and she groaned.

"That doesn't sound like the noise of a successful and happy lady," Chelsea commented, appearing beside her at the bar.

"I'm in trouble." Bekka blurted.

Chelsea placed the order for their drinks, then led Bekka over to an empty table at the side of the room. "What's going on Bekka?"

"I think I'm falling for Noah Fox."

"Yes. I can see that, thank you, I'm not blind. He is on the same page. I'm not sure what the problem is?"

"Where to start! He doesn't live here. He's only visiting for his sister's wedding."

Chelsea held up a hand. "He's also looking at real estate. That gives him a link to here. If it's love, distance shouldn't matter. Others have made those sorts of situations work too."

"That's just it. I'm..." her eyes slammed shut, her face scrunched tight, "I'm afraid to fall in love again, Chelsea. What if I fall all the way and he doesn't? What if he changes his mind and leaves?"

What if I'm more like my mom than I realized? She couldn't force those words past her lips.

"Bekka life is all about taking chances. What if he's the one and you don't try? Do you want to spend the rest of your life wondering?"

Bekka dragged in a lungful of air, then let it out in a huff. "I don't know. I'm worried that I don't know how to remain me and be in love. I fell asleep the other day and nearly missed a fitting appointment. Then last night I realized I hadn't placed a fabric order. My mind is constantly distracted by thoughts of him. I'm on edge waiting each morning, waiting to see him. It's like my body sighs in satisfaction just from having him nearby."

"Is that how you felt with Connor?"

That wasn't something Bekka had considered. She'd loved Connor, she knew that... but this felt different. Had that just been the residual infatuation of childhood love? This ran deeper. Allowing the thoughts to be verbalized, she could see that now. Her feelings for Noah were much, much deeper. That scared her. This deep dive was happening too quickly for her.

What if she lost her heart to him and he walked away with it?

"Bekka?" Chelsea prompted.

"No. My relationship with Connor was different. Noah… he's taken me by surprise."

"Then my advice—unsolicited, I know—is to just enjoy this time. Bekka, you're allowed to fall in love. It doesn't make you weak. We all get distracted when we're dating. You're just not used to feeling off-kilter."

Chelsea leaned in and hugged Bekka. She still didn't know what to do, but her frantic panic lessened with Chelsea's words. After Connor, she locked down on feeling anything for others, but perhaps her friend was right. She hadn't messed up her business, her career was still intact. Maybe she could just date Noah and enjoy the process.

"You're very quiet." Noah murmured, hooking a strand of Bekka's hair away from her eyes.

"Are we dating?" Bekka blurted out.

Noah raised a brow, caught off-guard. Since he'd arrived for their usual morning walk, Bekka had been quiet and distracted. They'd walked around the block and found a park to take Smooch to for a few games of fetch. The cavalier ran in little circles, collecting the stick they'd been throwing before he trotted back towards them.

"I thought so, yes." He chuckled, uncertainty hanging around the edge of Bekka's meaning. "I like you, Bekka. I want to see where this thing between us can go. Do you want that too?"

He reached out and took her hand, lacing their fingers together. Just holding her hand seemed to settle the unease that had jumped inside him at her words. He still didn't have any answers to how they could make this work long term, but he hoped they could work that out together.

"Yes. I do." She said after a moment. "I, just want to take things slowly."

"We can do that." Noah smiled.

The unmistakable ringtone of his phone sounded, breaking the moment. Fishing his phone out of his pocket, he frowned as he saw the seller's name come up on the screen.

"Sorry, I should take this." He apologized to Bekka who nodded, a slight puckering forming between her brows.

"Noah speaking."

"Noah. This is Max Steadwell. I have some bad news about the estate."

Noah stood, every muscle in his body locked tight as he walked away on autopilot. He listened as Max outlined that the family had reconsidered. They'd found another way to refinance so they could keep hold of the estate.

They wouldn't be selling.

Sorry for the inconvenience.

Noah swallowed back acid, his stomach lurching at this unwelcome news.

"Thanks for letting me know," he said and hung up, the phone almost slipping from his fingers.

He was numb. Biting his bottom lip, he grimaced and mentally cursed this bad luck. The estate on Long Island had been perfect. Everyone he'd shown his plans to had congratulated him on them—he'd finally talked his dad around to giving him the go-ahead.

His ducks had all been lined up, and now the first one had fallen over on the ground.

He turned, taking in the image before him. Bekka was whispering something to Smooch as she coerced the dog to give her the stick. She tossed it over to the side, laughing as the dog took off at high speed to chase the piece of wood before returning it to her to repeat.

Bekka seemed unsure about them. An air of uncertainty had come between them. He desperately ached to give Bekka whatever reassurance she needed, but he couldn't. He'd thought closing this deal would mean he'd have a definite time frame that he could give her. He could read her interest in her features and reactions to him, but he also saw the walls that sat there after what Connor had done. He needed more time to pull those walls down. Now he felt a little like he'd rowed them both up a creek and lost both the paddles. Did he tell her he lost the sale? There were other locations... he could look at those. Maybe he could find something else to lock in to keep him here.

He'd do that. He'd start searching again this afternoon. Call all the contacts he knew. Once he had another possible, he'd call his dad and inform him of the changes.

Once he had a definite timeframe for being here, he'd tell Bekka. They could sketch out some definite plans for their relationship. He wanted to take her on a vacation, to Italy, to all the places she'd always dreamed of. Once the wedding was over, they could make some plans and he'd cement in her mind that he was here to stay. He would not leave her, or back away from their relationship.

He was in this for good.

The next week passed in a blur. Noah arrived every morning to take her and Smooch for their daily walk, delivering her home and giving her a kiss that made her go weak in the knees and broke a little more of the wall around her heart.

Bekka started to believe. Maybe this was the real deal for her. They hadn't discussed their future, but instead of focusing on that, she tried to stay in the here and now.

Noah was hard at work on his plans for the expansion. She was finishing the last details on her latest collection, having made all the designs and completed details. Her scattered week had passed, and she felt more confident than ever. Her bookings were up and three separate bridal magazines had requested samples to put in their showcase issues.

She'd need to hire a few more assistants if this workload kept up. She sometimes used a local seamstress to help, but with how work was going, she'd be looking for someone full time.

The thought gave her a thrill.

Her career dreams were coming true.

On a whim, she texted her mother and said she hoped that things were working out with Tom and she couldn't wait for the wedding. Before pressing send she added on an offer to design a dress for her mom to wear.

It was time she let go of her past. Her mom might have a revolving door of love and men, but that didn't mean Bekka was like her.

The doorbell tinkled, and Bekka did a quick check she hadn't forgotten an appointment and walked to unlock the door.

Noah and Valerie stood on the doorstep. Their faces ashen.

"What's wrong?" Bekka stepped forward, instinctively reaching a hand to Noah's arm.

Valerie burst into tears, and Bekka's thought's jumped to the worst. "Come in." She hooked an arm across the other woman's shoulders and ushered her inside. Taking her straight through to the fitting room, she guided Valerie to the couch and sank down beside her.

"We've... postponed..." Valerie started, each word interrupted by heart-wrenching sobs.

Noah's face was white, and he kneeled in front of them. "Our mom just called. Dad's in hospital, he's had a heart attack. He's stable—for now—but they want to operate."

Bekka gasped. "Oh, my goodness. I'm so sorry." She pulled Valerie in tighter, giving the sobbing woman a proper hug. Her eyes shifted to meet Noah's. He looked wrecked, like the news had aged him ten years. She ached to comfort him too, but sensed he was unreachable just now, needing to stay strong for Valerie.

"We can't get flights until tomorrow morning, but Valerie and Arnold have postponed the wedding. She wanted to come tell you in person. We know you've worked around the clock to make her dress."

Bekka waved a hand, shocked the dress would even be a consideration. It wasn't going anywhere. Her mind had originally jumped to the conclusion that Valerie and Arnold must have broken up. That it was their father had her aching so much more inside.

"How is your mom?"

"Shaken, but... Dad's been having tests done for the past month. They knew his health wasn't what it should be."

Bekka frowned at the clipped edge creeping into

Noah's voice. "I'm sure they just didn't want to worry you…"

"By not telling us?" Noah stood now, energy emanating from his quick movements as he paced about the brief space, his hands on his hips. "I just feel hopeless. An idiot for not sensing something was up. It was staring me in the face!"

Bekka watched as he continued his pacing. "You'll go back and see him. Once you're back with your family, you'll feel better. He's still young."

Valerie shifted and sat up, wiping at her eyes. "Our grandfather died of a heart attack."

That news jolted Bekka. Noah had said their grandfather had died suddenly, but he hadn't specified how. She glanced at Noah and saw he'd gone a few shades paler.

"Grandfather was in his seventies. Dad's only mid-fifty. He's a fighter. I just wish they'd told us. This explains why he's been pushing me to take over, why he was happy that the Long Island estate sale fell through."

Bekka frowned. Did Noah just say the Long Island estate sale had fallen through? An eerie silence crept into her mind, her gaze finding the carpet. With each second that passed after his words, Bekka's stomach dropped further.

"Bekka?" Noah's voice crept into the void.

She startled when he took her hand, crouching before her. "I should have told you."

"It doesn't matter." She said on autopilot, shaking her head and forcing her lips into a small smile. "I'm sorry that you lost that venue. I know you had high hopes for it."

He sighed, his eyes dark with concern. "We have to go. There are a lot of calls to make to notify every one of the postponed wedding, but can I come back later tonight to see you?"

"Of course." He leaned in and placed a kiss on her cheek. She swallowed, as though the room was closing in on her. She held it together long enough to see them out. Closing and locking the door, she slid to the floor.

Why hadn't Noah told her?

What were they doing?

Goose bumps erupted on her arms, but all she felt was numb.

Her heart had broken seeing Noah's face and hearing about his father. Then with the news of his lost deal… it was enough to have her deciding.

They should end this before it became anything else. She choked back the acid that rose in her throat.

It was clear to Bekka that Noah needed to be back home with his family, with his dad, and helping in any way he can. She didn't know for sure, but she had a feeling Noah hadn't told her about the estate because it meant he'd lost his reason for staying here past the wedding.

They hadn't talked about it, but that conversation had been lurking in the background, like the proverbial elephant in the room that neither had wanted to bring up.

Now Bekka would.

This time she was getting out and protecting her heart for the right reasons. Noah should be with his family. If Bekka had ever been lucky enough to have a family like his she'd want that for her.

Now to work out how to barricade herself from the hurt she'd be subjecting herself to.

CHAPTER 14

Bekka had taken a cab to Brooklyn and bought cake. She'd stood in a line for more than an hour to order the last item the bakery had, which was a slice of salted caramel cheesecake.

It didn't seem like much of an offering, but it was all she could think of.

Smooch sensed her discomfort and had flopped down across her feet, not moving even to whine for dinner, which he normally would have had at least half an hour previously.

The clock ticked over to seven; the sound tearing Bekka from her staring into space. All afternoon she'd attempted work but hadn't been able to settle. Dread filled her every synapse at what she was about to do.

A knock sounded at the side door. Pushing to her feet, she walked over and opened the door to Noah. All six plus feet of gorgeous man that she wasn't destined to have in her future.

"Hi," he said with a tired half-smile, then leaned in to hug her. She drank in his smell.

"I bought cake." She shrugged, gesturing to the small kitchen table.

"Looks familiar. You went to Brooklyn?"

"Yes. Is there an update on your father?"

"He's stable. Mom's just gone home to shower and collect some clothes for dad. He's scheduled for a surgery mid next week."

"It must be hard, being so far away."

Noah shrugged. "Dad's strong. I spoke to the doctor who is an old friend of mine from high school. His outlook for Dad is positive. It was a shock, for sure, but it helped me understand a lot of what has been going on that hasn't made sense. It also solidified how I feel about you, Bekka. I know this is a lot, but I want you to come with me. I want you to come with us to Sydney."

Bekka's mouth dropped open.

He wanted her to move? To another country?

"Not forever." He clarified, concern flashing at the look that must have come over her face. "Just for a visit while Dad's in hospital. Think of it as a holiday. I know it's not Italy, but I'd still love you to see my country…"

"No," she blurted, her head shaking as though physically rejecting the word and all that came with it.

Noah's mouth turned down, a frown forming above those gorgeous green eyes.

"Bekka, don't do this. I love you. I want us to be together. We can't do that in separate countries and I need to be home right now for my family."

Love? Oh God, he loved her. Those three words attacked her resolve, fighting to break down her walls but she blocked them out, reminding herself of all the reasons why she had those walls. How she'd felt after Connor had walked away without even having the decency to speak to her himself. How witnessing her mother's continued broken hearts had hardened her own. How important it was to be with a loving family, which is what Noah deserved. Love... she wasn't ready to go there. This was for the best.

For both of them.

"I know you do. You need to be with your family and I would never stand in the way of that. But I can't come with you, Noah."

She walked over to the table and sat, pushing the single piece of cake forward to the seat that Noah took. His eyes narrowed in on her face, trying to pin down her gaze, but she couldn't meet his eyes. She'd weaken if she did. A clean break was better.

"Can't? Or won't?"

Bekka thought about that, but her answer didn't take long. "I won't. And I can't. My business is here. I cannot just go gallivanting off to the other side of the world on a whim."

"This isn't exactly a whim, Bekka. I'm laying all my cards on the table, right here, right now. I'm talking love, marriage… forever." He reached out and took her hand, but she snatched it away.

Her heart tripped at the last word. How often had her mother said those same words? *This time, Bekka, it's the real deal. It's forever.* But it never was. And going now, chasing a man halfway around the world, just felt like a mistake. She had feelings for Noah. True and deep feelings, but she promised herself she'd never give up anything precious to her again for a man. She'd learned that lesson with Connor. From her mom.

Bekka swallowed at the bitter twang developing in her mouth. "And what if you change your mind?"

"I won't!"

"So you say… now. But what if your feelings change? It happens… all the time. I nearly lost my business and dreams once before because of a promise of love, marriage, and forever. I'm sorry, Noah. I can't put into words how sorry I am, but I just… won't. You should go to your parents, be there for them. I'll be here. We can talk on the phone and maybe if you come back here, well, we could talk then—"

"Wait. So you're saying you'll be with me, but only if I stay here in New York?" His tone was harsh, but his face remained calm.

Her insides twisted so hard she wondered if they'd snap.

"Noah, don't make this any harder than it already is. This has been fun… but the timing just isn't right."

"You are breaking me here, Bekka," he sighed,

spreading his hands wide. "I have to go be with my family. Valerie postponed her wedding. My father is in hospital due to undergo open-heart surgery next week. I know how I feel. I love you. I want you to be with me… don't let me walk out of here without you. Please."

Bekka had never hated a situation so much in her life. She'd thought Noah's words the day he delivered the news of Connor calling off the wedding had hurt.

But this was so much worse.

Every fiber in her ached to say yes, but the words just wouldn't come out. She was petrified at the thought of just closing her shop and taking a risk on love. She was petrified of gambling with her heart. It might only be a visit to him, but to her, it was a line that if she crossed, she'd never come back from. Couldn't Noah see that?

She stared at him, her eyes pleading for him to understand. After a few moments, he let out a breath in a whoosh, the sound causing her to wince. He shook his head, then stood.

"Thank you for the cake. And… everything."

He then walked back outside without a second glance. Smooch stood whining at the door after it closed with a quiet click.

Noah walked out of her life, and she let him.

It was easier this way. Maybe he'd come back and they could be together again, but either way, she wasn't going to be the one in the weak position.

Too bad her fractured heart was telling her something else entirely.

"Noah and I broke up," Bekka said as she slid onto the stool in the milkshake bar. "We need not talk about it. I'm fine."

Chelsea raised her brows. Devon choked on the mouthful of milkshake she'd just taken.

"I think I'll order a slice of mud cake. I feel like cake. And chocolate." Bekka nodded, as though convincing herself, and flagged the waitress down to place her order.

Chelsea recovered first. "I think we should talk about it."

Devon nodded vigorously. "We definitely need to talk about it. What happened? You two were the bee's knees and on cloud nine."

"His father had a heart attack, he had to go back home to Australia to be with his family."

The two friends exchanged a look before focusing back on Bekka and speaking simultaneously. "Is he okay? Can't you go with him?"

"Noah asked me to. I ended the relationship with him." She mumbled.

"Ooookaaaay. So talk me through how you go from having a handsome man who cares about you, asking you to go with him to visit his sick father and instead you break up with him?"

"I couldn't go."

"Why?"

"Because…"

Every reason that came to her lips now seemed utterly silly.

Devon persisted. "Because why?"

"Because his life is in Australia."

Her cake was delivered, a giant mound of chocolaty heaven that only reminded her more of Noah. She picked up her fork, stabbing a piece, and forced it in. It may as well have been sawdust.

"Isn't he buying an estate here to turn into a hotel?" Chelsea asked with a frown.

"The sale fell through." She mumbled around a mouthful.

"I doubt that means he'll stop looking in the area though. You said his family business was looking to expand into this area?"

Giving up, Bekka put the fork down. "Yes, but that was before his dad had a heart attack. He should be home with his family now. They'll probably postpone any ideas for expansion."

"That still doesn't explain why you couldn't go with him."

"Because I feel like I'd be doing something my mom would do. I grew up promising myself I'd never change my entire life for a man. Something she did every other week!"

"Oh, sugar. You are not your mom. I've met no one with a heart more guarded than yours is. Taking a vacation with a guy you love is not changing your whole life for a man. And before you argue and say you don't love him, it's written all over your face." Chelsea said, her arms crossed across her chest.

"But I'd be walking away from my business. I can't do that."

"Heavens to Betsy. You're being crazy, girl. You look at your appointment book. You rearrange. You reschedule. You are allowed to take a vacation. He's only asking you to fly to Australia. He's not asking you to elope to the moon and give up your business."

Bekka swallowed, taking in both of her friends' faces that gaped back at her.

Could she do that? Could she just trust her feelings? More than that, could she trust Noah's?

As though gates had opened, remorse flooded in and Bekka gasped. She *was* being crazy. Hadn't she promised herself she'd give this a proper chance without letting her hang-ups get in the way? At the first hurdle thrown between them, she'd walked away. Noah wasn't Connor, and she wasn't her mother.

"I have to go." She blurted, pulling a few bills out of her purse and throwing them on the table before she dashed out of the shop, her friends cheers sounding behind her.

Bekka paced around her fitting room, her appointment book clutched in her hands. If she moved these three appointments and arranged extra help for the next two days with sewing the Smithson and Callahan dresses she could make this work.

If she just had the guts to try.

To trust.

She stopped walking and Smooch immediately laid across her feet. He'd need to go to one of her friends while she was away, but surely Devon or Chelsea could handle him for a few days? Or she could ask some of the other No Brides Club members. Many of them were dog lovers.

The only thing stopping Bekka from going after Noah and taking a chance on his word, was herself. The assuredness she'd felt after meeting her friends had dimmed a little, but deep down she knew they were right.

She was not her mom.

Noah was not Connor.

Chasing after Noah was not giving up her career.

Her phone beeped and she fished it out of the back pocket of her jeans. An unknown number flashed on the screen. Her heart leapt. *Noah? Was he calling from the plane or the airport?*

Clicking connect she brought the phone to her ear. "Bekka speaking," she rushed out.

"Bekka. It's Connor. Connor Chivers. It's been a long time."

Her heart dropped along with her shoulders. How often had she wished for him to call in those early days? To say he'd made a terrible mistake? Hearing his voice now just grated on her already taut nerves.

"Connor. I hear congratulations are in order." Her voice was level, her tone pleasant which she figured was quite a feat. It hit her then. There wasn't even the slightest wobble in her chest at hearing his voice, or saying his name. She genuinely didn't feel a thing for him anymore.

Because every ounce of her being was promised to Noah.

Every part of her soul ached for him. And she was letting him go, allowing her past to ruin her future whish she'd promised herself she'd never do all those years ago. Would she make the same mistake now? Noah was ten times the man Connor was, and she knew without a doubt now that letting Noah walk away would be one decision she'd regret for the rest of her life.

"Bekka?" Connor's voice was irritated.

"Sorry, I completely zoned out. Is this urgent? I have a plane to catch."

"Oh. Uh, I was just calling to apologize for how I ended things… and, um, for lying about Noah's involvement," Connor stuttered.

"It's in the past Connor. I'm only looking to my

future now." A giant smile broke across her face, happiness and elation filling her soul.

Connor paused, before continuing with a voice that sounded relieved. "Noah's a lucky guy. I'm really happy for you, Bekka."

"Thanks. I'm happy for you too." She hung up.

She was glad he'd called, and that the air was cleared on all facets from that time in her life. Connor was never the right man for her. But everything told her Noah was, and now she was finally seeing that for herself. She wasn't her mom. Making this decision to give love another chance didn't make her like her mom in a bad way.

It just made her human, and happy.

Noah sat beside his father's bed, taking in the monitors and tubes that ran in various directions. His father was asleep, but Noah had wanted to come straight here. He'd wanted to see him.

Every part of his body ached. He hurt inside and out, and yet he wasn't ready to give up on Bekka.

She was scared. He could see that. The timing was all wrong, but he didn't plan on letting this get between them. He knew with no doubt that he loved her. Being with her lit something within him. It was the same feeling he got when he looked at the perfect hotel location. It was a feeling of certainty. Of destiny.

If that took Bekka a little longer to realize well than he'd be there, urging her on. As soon as he could.

His father's hand stirred, bringing Noah's attention back.

"Hey Dad." He murmured.

His father's eyes blinked open, a little glazed before they focused and a small smile spread across his face. "Son. What are you doing back here?"

"Valerie and I came as soon as we could."

"Oh cripes. The wedding?"

"Postponed for now. They have it handled. Valerie went home with Mom to shower and change. Then she will come in. Why didn't you tell me you were feeling sick?"

"I didn't want you to worry." His father muttered.

"But this brought on the idea to step aside, didn't it? The push for me to take over the reins of the company?"

His father sighed. "Yes, it was. I didn't want you to feel blindsided. Like I was when your grandfather died. I was grieving and left with a business to run and honestly, I just didn't know what to do. I didn't want you to experience that same feeling of hopelessness."

Noah's chest ached. His father meant well, family was everything to him, and he'd always put them before his needs. Even if sometimes it was the wrong choice. "I know the business, Dad. You've made sure of that. But I think we need to sit down and have a proper discussion about the business. After you're better."

"You don't want to run the company." His father said, his voice resigned. A slight smile lifted one corner of his mouth.

"It's not that. You know I love the business, and yes, one day I see myself in that top role but for now, I really want to look after expanding it, not the day to day running and overseeing of the smaller details."

"You're the futures guy." His dad joked.

Noah shook his head, a slight grin in place. He squeezed his dad's hand. "Like I said, let's talk about it after your operation. But we're here, all of us."

"Where's your girl?"

Noah frowned, then rolled his eyes. "Mom been gossiping to you again, has she?"

"You know what she's like."

Seeing his dad smile helped each the ache in his chest a little. "She has a business to run. It was too much to ask her to drop everything and hop on a plane." A fact Noah had realized the minute he'd stepped onto the plane, but it hadn't made him regret putting the offer out there. He would call Bekka and apologize after he'd visited his father. He'd put her on the spot and he shouldn't have done that. Shock did funny things to a person. As much as his head had been desperate to be back in Australia with his family, his heart had stuck on the fact he'd be leaving Bekka behind. He'd wanted her with him.

He still did.

But he knew her career was important to her. He

was proud of all of her achievements. In an ideal world, he wanted to rearrange his business decisions to be with her. His goal of asking her to come on this trip wasn't to interfere with her business, just that he wanted her around. He wanted her to be a part of his family.

"I'm sorry about the Long Island estate. I know you had your heart set on that location." His father offered.

Noah cocked his head. "There will be others. I'd found another place that looked promising just before Mom called and we got the news you were in hospital. Honestly Dad, you really gave us a scare."

"I hope you've locked in a viewing."

"I, uh, haven't. I figured maybe I should put those plans on hold for now."

"No. Not on my account. Go call them now. And I'll expect pictures next time you come visit."

Noah shook his head. "You know you're not ready to give up the reins, don't you? The business is the blood that flows through your veins as much as this family is what keeps you breathing."

His father was every bit the company leader, even lying in a hospital bed surrounded by flowers.

"No. You're right." His dad chuckled. "I'm not ready to step aside. I see now that I was reacting in fear and pushing you in a direction you don't want. Now off you go. Make your phone calls and I'll see you tomorrow."

Noah patted his dad's hand. "Love you, Dad."

Bekka fidgeted with the hem on her shirt. It had taken her longer than she'd originally planned, but she'd made it. Her flight had just landed in Sydney, Australia. Now all she had to do was collect her bags, find her rental car, and navigate her way across a strange city to find Noah's parents' house. On the wrong side of the road.

Piece of cake.

Devon and Chelsea had been right. When she'd sat down and taken a proper look at her appointment book, she had easily rearranged five days off. It wasn't long, but she figured it would be enough. And well—it was better than being miserable, which is exactly how she'd been feeling from the moment the door closed behind Noah.

She had been so focused on her business and building a career, she'd not stopped to take a step back and live her life. She hadn't taken a vacation in goodness knows how long and nor had she allowed herself to take a chance. Noah walking back into her life had shown her that.

She'd lived more in the past month than she had in the past five years. Her life had become a rotation of designing and making collections, brides and career goals, and not once had she stopped to celebrate her wins.

Maybe it was time she did that and let go a little.

She could hire people to do some work instead of constantly working herself into the ground to control every last part. She could still do all the designing and fabric ordering and sit in on fittings where required. But she didn't need to be the only person behind Something Blue Bridal.

Building a career should be a goal, allowing her to live her life, not the only thing in her life.

Pushing Noah away had been a mistake, one she'd fix right now.

$\mathcal{A}$ breeze lifted and drifted past as the sun started to dip in the sky. Noah sat on the back verandah of his parents' house, looking out over the harbor. Golden glints reflected on the water's surface, and he pondered going out on the boat the following day.

The door squeaked a little, indicating someone was joining him before he spotted Valerie's brunette head. She held her phone, cocked between her ear and shoulder. One hand was pushing the door closed, and the other held two beers.

"Okay, bye." She said into the phone along with a few air kisses. Pulling the phone away from her ear, she hung up and then held a beer out to him. "For you."

"Cheers," Noah said, taking the beer and lifting it in a toast. "To Dad's health."

"I'll cheers to that," Valerie said on a sigh as she

dropped onto the seat beside him. "I'm glad the operation is out of the way and went according to plan. I couldn't sleep."

"Dad's strong. You heard the doctors. With a bit of exercise and healthier eating, he'll bounce back in no time. He needs to take it easy, to begin with, but I'm sure Mom will keep him on track."

"No doubt about that." Valerie laughed. "Arnold says hi."

"He's a great guy, Val. I'm sorry the wedding had to be postponed."

"Well, that's not your fault. And besides, it's only a wedding. What matters is having all the people I love there."

"You're lucky to have found Arnold. He's a good fit for you."

"A good fit?" she laughed, "you make him sound like a shoe."

"Trust you to think of shoes."

"You're lucky to have found Bekka." Valerie inserted after a bit, then took a deep swig of her beer.

"I tried calling her, but she didn't answer."

Noah took a deep drink from his own beer, the fizzy bitter liquid sliding down the back of his throat. It hit his empty stomach, reminding him he had skipped lunch. Bekka's no communication had hurt and created a fracture in his assuredness that they could work things out.

"She just needed some time."

Noah took another gulp, running the liquid around in his mouth before he swallowed. It went down sideways, Valerie's words sinking in.

"You've spoken to her," he spluttered, pinning her with his gaze.

"Yes. Just now."

"When? On the phone?"

"No, silly. In the kitchen."

Noah's heart jumped into his mouth and without replying he sprinted back into the house, nearly taking out the family cat in his enthusiasm to get through the door at the same time as Patch was trying to get out. Running into the kitchen, he skidded to a stop in the vast open space. His beer bottle nearly slipped out of his limp grasp.

There before him, at the extended wooden dining table, sat Bekka. Her hands cupped a mug of coffee. A large white box was before her.

"Bekka," he breathed. "You're here."

"Hi," she said in a small voice, the corner of her mouth lifting slightly. "I heard your dad's operation went well."

He nodded, having lost the ability to form words.

Valerie came to stand beside him, patting his chest. "It's customary to talk when someone flies halfway around the world to see you. Maybe you should take Bekka for a walk down to the beach?"

"Yes. Okay. Sure." He looked around, then stepped forward and put his beer down on the closest surface.

His hands were sweaty, which he wiped against his shorts. "If you want to?" he blurted, glancing at Bekka.

"I'd love to." This time the smile reached her eyes.

They walked down the private path to the beach. Bekka was wearing a long floaty dress, the straps thin and baring her shoulders. Her skin looked like fresh creamy silk compared to the dark curls that slid halfway down her back. She always seemed to wear her hair up or in a braid, but seeing it down made him itch to reach out and run his fingers through it.

"I can't believe you're here," he said, feeling idiotic the moment the words left his mouth.

"I can see you're surprised." She returned with a quick look over her shoulder.

The grass petered out; the sand taking over underfoot. They stopped as they exited the scrub and sand dunes that had hidden the water from view. Bekka gasped. "I can see why you love it here." Her voice was breathless, filled with awe.

"It's my parent's slice of heaven." He brushed his fingers against hers, encouraged when hers clung back, interlacing with his. "Are you game to walk down to the water?"

"Sure. The sand is so white. It feels amazing underfoot."

"Haven't you ever been to a beach?" he asked.

Bekka shrugged. "No. It's on my list. Which I can now check off."

"What else is on the list?" Noah asked, still unsure if

he wanted to dive in and ask why she was here. He almost worried that if he did, she'd turn out to be a mirage.

"Well. It's fairly long. I wrote it on the plane. Plenty of hours to kill on that trip!" her eyes slid to his from the side. "You know Australia is a *really* long way away, right?"

"I've done that leg of travel a few times, yes. It's not too bad. I guess it depends on what's waiting at the end that makes it worth it. So… the list?"

"Well." She pulled a handwritten piece of paper from a pocket in her dress. Unfolding it, she cleared her throat. "Sorrento."

"Interesting choice. If you're staying more than a couple of days, I'm sure I could arrange that."

"I have five days."

Noah nodded. "Then if that's top of your list, that's where we'll start. What else?"

"Swimming at the beach was next, but I think it's too cold for that."

"The forecast is meant to be nice for the next week, I'm sure we can find you a spot to swim further North."

"You might need to teach me to swim too."

Noah chuckled. "That may take over five days."

"Then I guess I'll have to come back."

"They have pools in America. I'm sure I could teach you there. Anything else?" He leaned over and saw the list was quite extensive. One thing that stood out for him was that his name featured prominently on the list.

"I notice a lot of your activities mention doing those things 'with Noah'."

"Yeah. I met this amazing guy, years ago, during college, and he recently came back into my life."

Noah stopped walking and turned Bekka to face him. The breeze lifted her hair and floated it back off her shoulders. The sun was only just peeping its golden glow above the horizon; the sky was awash with pink, orange, and golden hues. His heart rolled over at the sight.

Everything he'd ever wanted in his entire world stood before him. Bekka.

"An amazing guy, hey. And his name's Noah? That's a coincidence." He grinned.

Bekka's answering smile was brighter than the sun glinting behind her. "Not a coincidence. I came to tell you I'm sorry. I pushed you away, because I thought that was safer and less scary than trusting your feelings wouldn't change. Growing up, I know my mom loved me, but seeing her constantly on a rollercoaster of love with different men just scarred me. I took so long to let Connor in, that when that ended it was like the easy option to just hide from putting my heart on the line again. Which was easy to do until you came back."

"Bekka, I can't promise I'll never annoy you, or inadvertently hurt you, but I promise to love you. With all of my heart. Always."

"I promise to love you in return. And I promise to

try to not run scared whenever decisions get hard. I promise to trust you with my heart."

"Just so we're clear, I never planned to let you push me away forever. I have a flight booked back to New York on Saturday. If you let me know your flight details, I'll call the airline so we can fly together. We might have to go business class though, so we can get some work done."

"Work?"

"Yeah. I found a new location to expand the Luxury Fox boutique hotel group."

Noah stepped forward, his unoccupied hand pulling her in at the waist. She smelled of warm sunshine and gardenias.

"Where?" Bekka whispered.

"Long Island. Which means I'll be around, quite a bit."

"Perfect." She smiled, then leaned in and kissed him. Her lips were soft and melted against his. All of his dreams had come true. Lifting her in his arms, he swung her around, enjoying the giggle the move elicited. He placed her back on the sand. Her hair now had a halo from the last slip of golden light behind them before the sun dipped away completely.

Perfect.

EPILOGUE

Ten Months Later

Bekka smiled as Elaine presented the last design. The past few months had flown by in a whirlwind of work and discovering just how amazing her life could be now that she'd let go of a few issues from her past. Valerie's wedding had occurred exactly two months later than its original date, and the unveiling of Valerie's dress and subsequent pictures had skyrocketed on social media and in the bridal design world.

Something Blue Designs was now a team of four, with a full-time pattern maker, seamstress, and front of house assistant. Bekka was managing her hours much better and felt her designs had flourished with the extra downtime. She'd even been invited to show at next year's Milan bridal fashion show, and while she'd initially freaked out at saying yes, Noah had taken the option from her and declared they'd do it and tack on a well-needed holiday afterward.

"Elaine that's beautiful. You've brought the design to life." Bekka congratulated the pattern maker and wrapped up the meeting. She could hear Smooch yipping at the interconnecting door, which probably meant Noah had arrived. It was Thursday and her No Brides Club night, but Noah had insisted he wanted to pop in to see her before she went.

"Sounds like Noah is here," Serena giggled. The petite redhead was an absolute whiz on the sewing machine and Bekka wasn't sure how she'd managed without her to this point.

Waving off her new teammates, she walked over to the door. Unlocking it, a pleading doggy face greeted her, which she immediately turned into a cuddle.

"Noah?" Bekka called out.

"Out the back." His voice replied, floating in from the side door, which was propped open. Walking out the door and around the side, she entered her little courtyard, which she'd only just started using. There before her was a little table, set with a white tablecloth, red roses, and a single tapered candle. Noah kneeled before her on one knee.

Bekka frowned, her heart galloping faster than Smooch after a ball at the park. "What is this?" she gasped.

"What does it look like?" Noah chuckled, before clicking his finger.

Smooch wriggled, so she placed the dog down and he immediately ran to collect a small box that appeared in Noah's outstretched hand. Except instead of bringing it straight back to Bekka, Smooch shot off to the corner of the garden, chasing heaven knows what, and dropped the box on the way.

Bekka snorted, unable to keep the laughter in.

Noah stood and walked over, taking both her hands in his. "Bekka Arden, designer extraordinaire and love of my life, I'm attempting to ask you to marry me. I have spent all week working with Smooch to get him to help. So much for being my wingman." He rolled his eyes.

Giggling, she laid her forehead against his chest before looking up at the man she loved. "Probably for the best that your sister decided against using him in her wedding party."

"Most definitely. So?"

"So?" Bekka repeated, batting her lashes.

"Will you marry me?"

Bekka waited a beat, soaking up how perfect this moment was. "Yes. I will."

Noah let out a shout of glee, his face alight with happiness. Smooch reappeared at their feet, the small blue box in his mouth. Bending, Noah pried it out of the dog's mouth.

"If you don't like the ring, I can change it."

Bekka went up on her tiptoes and smacked her lips against Noah's. Her arms flung around his neck and she kissed him for all she was worth. "There's not a thing you do that I don't love, Noah Fox."

The ring was a classic white gold solitaire; the diamond sparkling brighter than Noah's gleaming eyes.

"Wow." Bekka breathed.

"Wow, good?" Noah grimaced.

"Wow, this is the most beautiful ring I've ever seen and I can't wait to try it on and show all the girls tonight."

His breath whooshed out. "Phew."

"I love you," Bekka whispered before kissing her fiancé.

The Tavern was bustling, people everywhere as was usual for a Thursday night. It had been a hot day, and it seemed everyone was keen to end it with a cool beverage in hand and amongst friends. Bekka twisted the ring on her finger, nerves making a sudden appearance.

She didn't know why she was nervous. These were her friends, and so many of them had found their own true love since joining the club. Deciding it was maybe more excitement than nerves, she stepped into the dining room and spotted her friends immediately.

Walking over, she stood at one end of the table,

grinned, and held up her hand, waiting for them to spy the sparkling diamond.

Chelsea was the first. Squealing she jumped from her place at the other end of the wooden dining table, and ran around to envelop Bekka in a hug.

"He proposed!"

"And I said yes!"

After all the others had congratulated her, Bekka and Chelsea headed to the bar to order dinner.

"I think I'm going to just order dessert," Bekka said, looking at the glass cabinet. She couldn't resist the array of delicious looking cakes.

Chelsea's eyes widened in theatrical shock. "Dessert instead of dinner? Who are you?"

"I'm a changed woman." Bekka giggled. "And I'm making time for cake."

Maybe she'd order a second piece later and take it home to Noah. After all, he was the one who taught her to trust in love again.

The End

PREVIEW OF TAILORED FOR HER PRINCE

SNEAK PEEK ...

If you enjoyed No Time for Daydreams, read on for a sneak peek at book 1 of my Stenish Royals Series. Sweet Royal Romance at it's finest.

Chapter 1

If the prince kept moving, Eva would end up measuring more than just his inseam.

Mentally rolling her eyes, she jotted down an adjustment before taking a step back to assess the slim line of the pants.

"I think they are too long." His cheeky tone interrupted her thoughts as he shifted his right leg, kicking out the hem. *Was he making fun?* She flicked a glance at the clock—half an hour of miniscule changes, yet the suit still evaded perfection to her trained eye.

Plucking a dress pin from between her lips, she bent to adjust the right leg hem a fraction. Standing again, Eva checked her previous fit notes. The jacket lapels needed to be slimmed down and the cuff buttons should be contrasting. Noir silk perhaps, to match the Armani shirt the prince had brought to the fitting. Perfection was Eva's middle name, and she had to get this outfit right. The company, and Gramps, were counting on her.

"You know I was only joking, right?" Felix said.

Eva returned Prince Felix's grin with a nod. After one appointment, a few things were clear to Eva. The prince was a born flirt, with a body made to drive women to distraction. Broad shoulders held the fine wool Eva draped across them beautifully.

They did nothing for Eva.

Tapping a blossom pink fingernail to her mouth,

she took a slow walk around the form before her, analysing every seam, every stretch of fabric. He'd selected the silver-grey superfine and Eva approved. The tone was brought to life by his suntanned skin and ash blonde hair. With the black silk shirt, and slim tie, he'd be a shoo-in for a James Bond lookalike, which was the style of suit he'd asked for. God knew why.

"You know, Eva, if I may call you that… you're hard to figure out."

"Why's that, Your Highness?"

"Felix, please." The prince captured her hand, bringing her focus to him. The move gave her pause, uneasiness creeping into her stomach at the unwanted touch. "I'm not your prince, after all. Tell me about yourself?"

"What would you like to know, Your Highness?" Eva wasn't trying to be evasive, but she couldn't fathom what he wanted to hear. "I'm a Savile Row Tailor, my grandfather is Ernesto James. He taught me everything I know."

Her Gramps was one of the best in the business, his reputation impeccable. Eva made sure every piece of work she did lived up to that standard. Fitting for a prince from the small Northern European country of Stenaco might be a first but she planned to act just as she did with every other client. Cordial, polite and extremely professional.

"I see I'm not going to win the battle of name

etiquette, am I? Something to work on next time, perhaps." The prince's left eyebrow rose as his eyes searched Eva's.

Keeping her expression carefully neutral, Eva said nothing.

"You're tougher than you look, Miss James."

"You may call me Eva, Your Highness."

"Finally, she consents to something. Tell me what you do when you're not tailoring to the high and mighty? Do you have hobbies? A boyfriend? Young children dressed in splendidly made clothes?"

The right corner of Eva's lips lifted. "No, Your Highness, no children or significant other. I have a small group of close friends from my time at design school, and in my spare time, I read." Removing her hand, Eva moved over to her sewing bench to make a few notes on the order.

"See? Now that wasn't so hard, was it?" The twinkle was back in his eyes.

"Of course not, Your Highness." Eva double checked the notes she'd written. Lapels, finish lining, additional inside pocket, buttons—it was all there. "I believe I have everything required. Thank you for coming in. I'll finish these today and have them delivered first thing tomorrow." Bowing her head slightly, Eva struggled to remember if she should curtsy or not before leaving the room. She'd never fitted royalty and wasn't sure on the protocol. Would the rules for Stenaco even be the same as they were in England?

Get a grip, Eva. Stop causing yourself undue stress and overthinking things.

The request to see Prince Felix of Stenaco had only arrived three days prior. Eva had done some shuffling, knowing a new client, one with royal lineage, could be the difference she needed to ensure her gramps' business didn't falter. The work would see her hand-stitching until three a.m. again, but it would be worth it. Every stitch, every line perfectly crafted by hand, every minute detail would put her one step closer to success.

The prince's mouth lifted in a small quirk. *Damn.* She guessed her awkwardness had shown.

"One more moment of your time, Eva, if you don't mind." The prince's words didn't offer refusal as an option.

Eva hooked her hands together, standing ramrod straight. *Oh God. Please don't ask me on a date.*

He shrugged out of the partially sewn pieces of jacket. Stepping down from the fit dais, he moved leisurely to hang the fabric on the mannequin guarding the corner of the room. Eva tensed, waiting for him to speak his request.

"How would you feel about taking a royal appointment? We have tailors in Stenaco, but I'm looking for someone ... different. After today, I know I don't need to see more of what you produce to know you're that person."

Eva opened her mouth to reply, but no words formed. She'd been expecting a proposition, but not a work-related one. *Thank goodness!* Her shoulders sagged with relief that she wouldn't have to navigate a tactful decline. The tightness in her chest eased, freeing her mind and mouth. Work-related offers she could handle.

"Your Highness, if I may speak plainly, your offer comes as a shock." Eva chose her words carefully, widening her eyes to prove her point and gain herself a little thinking time. She averted her gaze as the prince changed back into his own clothes. He obviously felt no shame swanning around half-naked before a woman he'd only met twice.

Taking a deep breath, Eva exhaled slowly, running her hands along the crisp tucks of her tailored indigo pants. She'd never aspired to be anything other than a tailor, to keep the business alive in an ever-dying industry. Sure, she had dreams, but they were hidden. Locked away in her design books.

Besides, she couldn't leave her gramps, not when he was sick. She was needed here to keep the flailing business ticking over. Of course … a royal appointment would be amazing, maybe even a significant enough income to cover their expenses until she could work out a way to increase business, but what would her gramps do without her here? She couldn't possibly even consider this request, could she?

Prince Felix lifted her chin with a single finger, his

slate-blue eyes capturing hers. She swallowed, his proximity a little unnerving. Something about his eyes were familiar, reminding her of … *no don't go there Eva.*

"Just have a think on it," Felix murmured. "I'll have my assistant drop over the offer later today."

The door whooshed open behind her.

"For God's sake, Felix, do you have to paw at every unsuspecting female you meet? We're late." The voice slammed into her present like it was yesterday. Had she conjured him?

Ignoring the goosebumps that rippled along her bare arms, she craned her neck over her shoulder. Her brain disconnected from the rest of her body, shock ripping through every synapse.

Five years weren't enough to erase the thoughts and feelings that tumbled into her soul when she locked eyes with the man who stood commanding the doorway of her fitting room.

"Henrik." His name was a whisper on her breath.

Eva's shock turned to confusion at the sight of two burly, suit clad men flanking Henrik. They looked a lot like bodyguards.

"Nothing wrong with appreciating beauty when one finds it, brother dear. Miss Eva James is a fine talent. Her hands create magic. Your own style could use updating; perhaps you should try her wares."

Wait, brother? *Henrik is Felix's brother... He's royalty?* Her knees sagged as question after question tumbled through her mind. *Why hadn't he told her he was royalty?*

Was that why he disappeared? Was he ordered away? Stop! She needed to focus.

Henrik's azure gaze bore deep into her own. Her body turned of its own accord as his measured gait drew to a standstill before her.

"Miss James, it's a pleasure." His hand was planted before her, waiting for her acceptance.

Was he kidding? Did he not recognise her?

"Eva, dear, it's customary to shake a hand when presented. Especially the hand offered by his Royal Highness, Crown Prince Henrik of Stenaco." Prince Felix's words seemed far too casual to Eva. Like he knew.

Eva averted her gaze to the seam of Henrik's left shoulder before taking the hand before her. Her gut churned with unease. Executing a curtsy she hoped was satisfactory, she then dropped his hand like it was molten lava. *Crown Prince Henrik of Stenaco.* The words swam before her, her brain fuzzy as it tried to comprehend their meaning. The Henrik she'd known had never mentioned anything that even hinted at being royal, that he was in line to rule a small country. Hell, she thought he'd been a poor student like her, it was certainly how he'd acted.

Finding an inner strength, Eva's eyes flew back to his, searching, imploring him for any sign of recognition. How could he have forgotten her? Their time together, though short, had meant so much to her ...

Deep down, she'd held on to the belief it had meant something to him too.

His lips became a flat line. Shuttered eyes met hers for a second then travelled over her shoulder. "Time to go, Felix. The limousine is waiting."

And that was that. The two men left with nothing more than a cursory nod from Felix, their bulky black shadows close behind.

Eva had dedicated hours of her life imagining the perfect scenario where she ran into Henrik. She often thought of all the reasons he'd never shown that night. She'd always shied away from the notion he'd been using her, that she'd misread his feelings. Had she just been a fun conquest to him? Something to joke about when he'd returned to his real life, how he'd duped a silly woman into falling for him without having to use his title? Of course, she'd made that pretty darn easy for him. More fool her.

On autopilot, Eva moved about the shop, flipping the closed sign and locking the front door. Placing one foot in front of the other, she trudged upstairs, seeking comfort from the worn leather of her sewing chair which sat nestled under the large-scale windows of the sitting room. The soft snores of her gramps were a relief, zipping through her chest. *At least I don't have to explain my closing early.* Eva stared at the gilt-edged fireplace that normally offered warmth and comfort, feeling numb. The light was too bright; the rug was so happy; the air was too fresh. Eva moulded her slim form into a ball, hoping she could roll away to the land of nothingness.

Five years hadn't diminished the invisible draw she felt whenever Henrik was nearby. His height still towered over hers, causing a feeling of fragility and femininity. His lips still looked like every taste of heaven. Eva closed her eyes and let the memories wash over her.

Eva had been roped into taking a week off to celebrate her twenty-first birthday. Her friends had organised a miniscule apartment in Vernazza, part of the picturesque Cinque Terre region on Italy's coast. After a variety of harried train trips, with the last leg completed on a seemingly directionless bus, the girls had arrived tired and hungry. They'd been warned about the stairs required to reach their apartment so had decided to cure their hunger before attempting that feat.

Eva had been in a cloud of wonder since she'd stepped foot in the seaside village. The sun setting on the horizon, the vivid primary-coloured boats floating in the bay like little pieces of candy. Wafts of rich tomato and freshly caught fish enveloped her senses, enough to have her walking into a complete stranger. His strong arms had captured her fall, finding their way to her hips. She'd drowned in his sparkling eyes whilst he'd attempted to hold back his mirth.

Eva remembered how she'd felt disconnected, her limbs refusing to move from his grasp. Her lips had tingled from a need she'd never experienced before. Her already heightened senses had short-circuited from his touch. They'd only exchanged one word—his bemused warning for her to be 'careful' before he'd set her upright and walked off. She should have heeded his words.

Eva had eaten her meal, her eyes searching of their own accord for a certain pair of blue orbs. She'd barely remembered making her way up to the apartment before falling into a restless slumber.

Waking at dawn, unable to quiet the urge to go searching, she'd found herself once again down by the water. The night before, the area had been filled with wine and laughter; that morning held nothing but silence. The gentle lap of water offered a soothing contrast to the fast beat of her heart.

He sat on the rock wall as if waiting for her.

For five days, Eva had avoided her friends and fallen headlong into the world of Henrik. He'd professed to be a student, on a break from University. Away with friends just like her.

Every moment together had been filled with molten kisses and sighs, with only snippets of real life offered. Eva had never experienced that need before, the complete satisfaction from a physical connection.

She'd been the one to request they keep it light, no sharing of personal details, except even knowing next to nothing she'd fallen in love with him. When he'd asked her to meet him, the night before she was due to leave, she'd hoped it was to exchange details. A request to continue their affair, turn it into a real relationship.

Eva had waited. Three long hours as the sun vanished, and the moon exposed her foolishness.

Now she had proof that Henrik was never who she'd thought he was. And she was nothing to him at all —not even a memory.

Rain hammered against the limo's shaded windows, matching Prince Henrik's mood perfectly. Typical bloody London.

He shouldn't have come.

His brother had been acting weird lately, and this just proved he was up to something. If he hadn't agreed to collect Felix, he'd have never laid eyes on Eva again. She was a weakness he couldn't have in his life. A wish he could never fulfil.

"You're very quiet, brother dearest. Something on your mind?" Felix's words hung in the air, pointed with his knowing tone.

"No." Henrik's response was crisp. A silent request to cease any further questioning.

He adopted a bored expression and turned to face his younger brother. Envy washed through him. How nice it must be to have the title without the pressure. Whilst the brothers shared many similar physical traits, they couldn't be more polar opposites in personality.

Felix's laid-back propensity for fun deeply contrasted Henrik's tightly held emotional reins. It was expected of him. From as early as he could remember, he knew he had to be just that bit better, more reserved, utterly calm, emotionless. The last time he'd let his true passions shine had been in Italy. Where he'd been able to truly be himself and immerse himself in the beauty and wonder that was Eva.

Then he'd received a sudden order to return home and watch his mother quietly die, her final words reminding him he had no place living a life of passion. Of love.

"So, are you staying at Lady Sophia's estate whilst we're in town?" Felix asked with an edge in his voice.

Henrik glanced over, taking in Felix's pinched features before his trademark lazy grin reappeared. What was that about? Henrik wondered if he'd imaged the look before dismissing the thought. "No, Sophia is visiting with friends in Monaco. I said I'd see her at the ball next month."

"Next month?" Felix's incredulous laugh followed his words. "That's some romance you got there, brother."

Henrik offered no response.

He knew the rumours circulated that he'd chosen Lady Sophia to be his wife. He and Sophia had gotten a kick out of reading the delighted tales of royal romance and speculation on when the engagement would be announced. It would have to be soon; the pressure for him to marry was mounting, and Sophia was on the same page. Like him, she understood that duty came before freedom. They'd been friends a long time, and Henrik knew it would never be a great love story, but their betrothal would hopefully prove companionable.

His hands clenched at the thought. A burst of anger at his fate which he quelled with the ease of having done so a thousand times. His life was not his own, and he had long ago accepted that. It didn't mean he had to like it.

The car slowed to a stationary position. Not waiting for his bodyguard, he flung open his door, rain slashing across his face.

Unfolding his tall frame, he strode towards the palatial entrance of The London. Frank, the taller of his two ever-present bodyguards, attempted to shield him from the rainy skies with an umbrella. Pausing, Henrik let his gaze wander around him. Black skies, black-suited bodyguards, black umbrella. Black mood to seal it all. The thought had his lips twitching in a grimace before he resumed his march to the hotel lobby. Not stopping to acknowledge the manager who dashed towards him, or waiting for his brother, he took refuge in the elevator. Shoving his hands in his pockets, he let his lids shutter closed over tired eyes. Soaking in his five seconds of alone time, knowing his other set of bodyguards would be waiting by the penthouse doors, he gave in to temptation and let his mind drift back to Eva.

The years hadn't diminished her exquisite beauty. She was slimmer than he remembered, her natural grace clear in her movements. Her chocolate hair hung in straight locks, brushing against her shoulders. It was shorter than when he'd last seen her, when it had fallen in a glossy cascade down her back. Today she was dressed to work, crisp buttoned-up clothing hiding what he knew to be delectable curves. He could still bring to mind the sweet taste of her skin, her soft smiles and wondrous coffee-brown eyes. Those eyes had rattled him with confusion today when he'd pulled out his best acting to cloak their previous interactions.

He could have acknowledged knowing her, but really, what was the point? If they'd been alone, he knew he would have crumbled. His brother's presence had helped him stay strong. An ache settled in his chest at the deception, but it was for the best; she deserved better than him.

Ding. The elevator slid smoothly to a stop, drawing a line through his reminiscing. The silver doors slid apart to reveal his royal assistant impatiently tapping his foot, a tablet glued to his left hand as he furiously stabbed at the screen.

"Your Highness, your father has requested I review your schedule for the next few days. He has a few additional requests on your time whilst you're in London."

Stefan gave a brief bow, then immediately launched into a quick step to match Henrik's. The man didn't draw breath before ticking off various new luncheon requests, breakfast meetings, and a formal dinner at the embassy. An overly full schedule would prove a welcome distraction from his thoughts on a certain brunette. He supposed he should ask Lady Sophia if she'd be available to fly in for the dinner but discarded the idea. Felix could come along. His brother's ability to turn over happy conversation with a stone would save Henrik from the boredom he knew would await them both. He stopped walking. Would he have been the more outgoing and personable son had he not been first born?

"Sir?"

Henrik heard his assistant but didn't answer, instead taking in his surroundings. He stood in the spacious sitting area of the penthouse, owned by the royal family especially for state visits like this. It was elegant, and to him, a home away from home. It had plush carpet, in parts covered by red and gold embroidered rugs—pieces that had been brought over from Stenaco. The furniture had been commissioned, handcrafted, and approved by his mother. She'd loved decorating; it had been her passion. Her one outlet. She'd had the biggest smile when she saw the final version of this armchair ... it took her an age to choose where to place it. Moving it around to five different spots before setting it so it faced the windows. He ran a hand along the soft, slightly worn, fabric. He saw her in his mind, her expression carefree and filled with true happiness as she sat in this very spot. So different from her normally guarded face.

Why was he torturing himself with so many memories today?

Moving to the wall of windows, he gazed out at the cityscape that surrounded him. The London Eye sat square in his vision, its tiny bubbles moving in a slow circle, affording others a similar view to what he was seeing now. His country was not as big as England; its capital city, Geravia, was nowhere near as populated. But he loved his home, loved his country.

"Sir?" Stefan asked, concern entering his tone.

"Yes, Stefan." His words sounded dull even to his ears.

"Sorry, sir, but yes to which?"

He had no clue what Stefan was talking about. He turned towards his assistant, his right eyebrow quirked in question. Stefan fidgeted with the switch at the side of the tablet. A worried frown showed on his face as he opened his mouth a few times.

"Stefan, I have no idea what you are asking. Please accept my apologies. I was not listening." Henrik sank into the lush claret coloured leather couch. The smooth coldness enveloped his form, leaving him wishing the marble fireplace was lit.

Stefan's frown deepened.

"Is everything all right, Your Highness? Shall I have a doctor summoned?"

"No, Stefan. I'm not sick." *Not a sickness that a doctor could cure, anyway.* "Please start again. I promise this time you have my full attention."

Stefan's look was dubious.

"Full attention, Stefan. You have my word."

Hooking his left ankle across his right knee, Henrik focused his mind. He'd had his five minutes of distraction.

Time to go back to being the crown prince.

Grab your copy of Tailored for Her Prince (The Stenish Royals 1)

THE STENISH ROYALS

(Sweet Royal Romance)

#0.5 Finding A Forever Love (Novella prequel - available as a free download)

#1 Tailored for Her Prince

#2 Her Convenient Playboy Prince

#3 Guarding His Runaway Princess

FOUR SEASONS OF ROMANCE

(Sweet Novella Reads)

#1 Cherry On Top (Spring)

#2 A Kiss for Christmas Eve (Winter)

SINGLE TITLES

(Steamy contemporary romance)

Loving Lucas

NO BRIDES CLUB

(Multi-author Sweet Contemporary Romance)

No Time for Daydreams